*"Who lo*

She looked surprised by the question, one she clearly had not asked herself.

Lightning struck Fletcher then, an electric shock that rearranged a lifetime of isolation. His noble intentions to leave her alone burned up and blew away.

Closing the last bit of distance between them, he raised an arm and his fingertips brushed her cheek; it was so soft a snowflake would have slid right off.

Fletcher moved slowly, giving her time to stop him. And praying that she wouldn't. In his entire life he couldn't remember a moment when he'd wanted so badly to give rather than take.

Dear Reader,

I have a hidden talent: I can whistle the theme songs to *The Andy Griffith Show, I Love Lucy, Here Come the Brides, The Mary Tyler Moore Show* and *My Three Sons.* I would gladly move to Mayberry (if it existed, and I could convince my family to live without a mall). Remember how those great old shows depicted community? Neighbors were friends, friends were family and people's foibles made them more lovable.

Working on a new series, I wanted to create a world in which men and women fall in love with help from their friends and neighbors, where people laugh a lot and cry a little, and where you, the reader, can feel like one of the family.

It's my hope that your time in Honeyford will give you that delicious life-is-good feeling.

Welcome to Honeyford. Welcome home!

*Wendy Warren*

# THE COWBOY'S CONVENIENT BRIDE

## *WENDY WARREN*

# SPECIAL EDITION®

Published by Silhouette Books

**America's Publisher of Contemporary Romance**

SILHOUETTE BOOKS

ISBN-13: 978-0-373-65550-2

Recycling programs
for this product may
not exist in your area.

THE COWBOY'S CONVENIENT BRIDE

Visit Silhouette Books at www.eHarlequin.com

**Printed in U.S.A.**

**Books by Wendy Warren**

Silhouette Special Edition

*Dakota Bride* #1463
*Making Babies* #1644
*Undercover Nanny* #1710
*\*The Boss and Miss Baxter* #1737
*Once More, At Midnight* #1817
*†The Baby Bargain* #1820
*\*\*The Cowboy's Convenient
    Bride* #2067

\*Family Business
†Logan's Legacy Revisited
\*\*Home Sweet Honeyford

Silhouette Romance

*Mr. Wright* #936
*Romantics Anonymous* #981
*Oh, Baby!* #1033
*Her Very Own Husband* #1148
*Just Say I Do* #1236
*The Drifter's Gift* #1268
*The Oldest Virgin in Oakdale* #1609

---

## WENDY WARREN

lives with her husband, Tim, a dog, a cat and their daughter, Elisabeth, near the Pacific Northwest's beautiful Willamette River. Their house was previously owned by a woman named Cinderella, who bequeathed them a gardenful of flowers they try desperately (and occasionally successfully) not to kill, and a pink General Electric oven, circa 1958, that makes the kitchen look like an *I Love Lucy* rerun.

A two-time recipient of Romance Writers of America's RITA® Award for Best Traditional Romance, Wendy loves to read and write the kind of books that remind her of the old movies she grew up watching with her mom— stories about decent people looking for the love that can make an ordinary life heroic. Wendy was an *Affaire de Coeur* finalist for Best Up and Coming Romance Author of 1997. When not writing, she likes to take long walks, settle in for cozy chats with good friends and sneak tofu into her husband's dinner. She always enjoys hearing from readers and may be reached at P.O. Box 1208, Ashland, OR 97520.

# Chapter One

Pajama-clad and sock-footed seven-year-old Will Dobbs raced across a scarred pine hallway, skidded a sharp left into his room and took a flying leap onto the mattress. He sat cross-legged with his arms wrapped around his chest, his teeth chattering like castanets. "I'm f-f-f-f-freezing!"

As urgently as an outlaw with a posse at his heels, five-year-old Orlando dove into bed beside his big brother, shaking his legs with enough force to make the headboard rap against the wall. "M-m-me t-t-t-too! I got goose bumps all over me."

"My lips are frozen."

"My tongue is. Listen—I ca' har'ly talk."

Refusing to be outdone by his younger sibling, Will rose to his knees. "I'm so cold, I'm pissin' ice cubes."

"William Romeo Dobbs!" At the sound of their mother's voice, both boys made bug eyes at each other and scrambled beneath the sheets.

Claire hustled to her sons' bed, a tattered but thick blanket folded in her arms. She stared down at them. "Where on earth did you learn that expression?"

Will mumbled from under the sheet. "Sorry, Mom."

"Well, I should say." After an admonishing glare for good measure, she shook out the cover, spreading the thick wool across the bumps and angles of their small bodies. "Besides, it's hardly a contest. Y'all are both human Popsicles. I better warm you up quick or I'll find two icicles in bed tomorrow instead of little boys." She began to tuck them in with exaggerated urgency, making them giggle.

Will offered another exaggerated shiver, mostly, his mother hoped, for effect. "Is Oregon always cold?"

"Nope. By summer it'll be so hot we'll wish for a frost."

"Mom?" Pulling the covers up to his chin, Will frowned. "Are we staying here forever?" He watched carefully for her response.

Gazing down at him, Claire felt a rush of love and regret that made her heart feel like a sponge with the water squeezed out. Sitting on the bed, she let their hazel gazes settle into each other. Will was the one of her offspring that most resembled her, particularly in his tendency to fret about the future. Smoothing his wheat-colored bangs, she tried to sound like a woman with a great plan. "I expect to live here for years and years, Will. I figure you and your brother and sister will live here until you go off to college. Then I hope you'll come home for Thanksgiving and Christmas." She went nose to nose with him. "At least you better, or I'll bake your favorite pies and eat them all myself."

Orlando popped up in bed as if his spine were a spring. "I'm gonna stay with you, Mom. Me and my wife are gonna live here and drive you around in our car."

"You gotta get a job before you buy a wife and car." Will rolled his eyes and tugged at the blanket his brother had pulled off. "That's how come I'm going to college." He nodded importantly at Claire, who nodded importantly back. She'd done a thorough job of impressing upon her eldest that he would the first Dobbs to go to college, not to mention the first to graduate from high school.

Orlando ignored them both, his unleashed enthusiasm making him bounce on the bed. "I'm gonna work in a mine like Daddy. I'm gonna wear a hard hat with a light on it and big boots for my feet."

The sweetness of the evening drained abruptly for Claire, replaced by a nausea she had grown used to over the past year. Before moving lock, stock and barrel to Oregon, she, her boys and their father had lived in eastern Kentucky, in a town where any man worth his salt worked as a mountaintop miner. Arlo Dobbs had definitely been worth his salt. He'd lied about his age and gone to work for the mining company when he was only sixteen. By eighteen, he'd saved enough money to rent a home and buy a wedding band, and the day he'd asked Claire to marry him, he'd looked as proud and notable as a millionaire.

Glancing out the rectangle of window above her sons' bed, Claire wished she could see a star through the thick cloud cover. She needed a reminder that heaven could sometimes be seen right here on earth. She'd become Arlo's wife before she'd been able to vote and had never regretted it. He had been a man easy to love and easy to honor, but she didn't want any of their babies following his footsteps.

*Or mine, either.* Her jaw tensed. Somewhere under that great big sky was a kinder, better life. She intended for her children to have their fair share of it.

"You don't look happy."

Will's worried voice jerked Claire to her present. She smiled to ease her boy's fears. "I'm always happy when I'm with you and Orlando and Rozzy. I was just thinking about how I've got to sew the curtains for your window."

"And you don't like to sew?" Orlando guessed, up and jumping on his knees now, making the tired mattress sag.

"It's not what I'm best at." Gently but insistently, Claire pushed him down to his pillow.

"What are you best at?"

She pretended to have to think about it. "Good-night tickles." She dove for their ribs, eliciting easy laughter from Orlando. When Will chortled, too, Claire counted herself a success and left her sons to what she hoped would be a good night's sleep.

Trudging across the short hallway to the room she shared with her baby girl, Rosalind, Claire felt too stiff and tired to be twenty-five, too young to be a widow—but life hardly ever asked permission before it changed on a person.

There were plenty of risks associated with working in a mine, but Arlo hadn't succumbed to those. He'd died in a single-car accident along a winding road on the way home from work. At the time, Claire had had two children under six and a baby ready to be born. There hadn't been any family or education to fall back on, and she'd begun to think God might be teaching her a lesson when life had shifted again and suddenly she'd been back in His good graces.

Her great-aunt Faylene on her mother's side had passed on at the comfortable age of ninety-two, bequeathing Claire this two-bedroom, one-bath, totally paid-off house about sixty miles east of Oregon's central corridor. Except for Arlo's 1980 Oldsmobile Cutlass Supreme with cruise control, it was the first time Claire had owned anything bigger than a suitcase. Such a windfall—a house that was all hers with no questions asked and roomfuls of furniture to go with it—had sent her straight to her knees in gratitude and relief.

Walking softly to the crib where her eleven-month-old

slept, Claire gazed at the fair, Ivory-soap skin Rosalind had inherited from her father. Rozzy would never know Arlo, and the boys were still so young…. The details they remembered now would blur until the time came when their daddy was a memory and no longer a feeling. It killed Claire to think of it.

Putting two fingers to her lips, she pressed a kiss softly against Rosalind's cheek then headed downstairs, flipping off lights on her way to the living room. There, she checked the thermostat: fifty-one degrees if she squinted, and it was only early November; winter in eastern Oregon had not even begun.

Belligerently overriding the financial fears that never left her now, she shoved the thermostat up a good ten degrees. Letting her babies turn blue in their beds was not part of her plan.

She needed a job, and she needed it yesterday. She'd barely driven across the Oregon border before she'd started looking for employment, but her search had left her bone dry. Until today. This afternoon, she had spied her first golden ray of hope—an employment notice in the local paper.

*Two years' guaranteed employment for an honest, hard-working woman. Can you cook, muck a stall, bake a pecan pie? Integrity and loyalty a must to join the team at Pine Road Ranch. Apply in person. 120056 Old Pine Road. Benefits.*

Heart skipping with excitement, Claire had clipped the ad and stuck it to the refrigerator using one of her aunt's "Faith, Hope and Love" magnets for good luck. Every chance she'd gotten tonight, she'd reread it.

*Pine Road Ranch.* It sounded like the kind of operation that had been around for years, would be around for years to come. This could be the job that saved her.

Claire didn't hold with being disrespectful to her elders,

but before Arlo there hadn't been a Dobbs in all of Willow Hills, Kentucky, who'd worked an honest day in his life. Her family hadn't been much better. The one thing she had made Arlo swear to before she'd agreed to marry was that their kids would feel secure and protected. Never, ever would their own parents give them cause to lower their eyes in shame.

She intended to have that job. Since cooking was a skill she'd perfected in grade school, Claire decided to give the folks at Pine Road Ranch samples to make their mouths water for more.

In her kitchen, the cow-shaped clock Aunt Faylene had hung between the tile counter and the nicked, cream-painted cabinets read seven thirty-five. Time to get to work. There were cinnamon rolls to ice, homemade-jam cookies and a butter-soft egg bread to bake, plus a chicken she planned to roast with carrots, pearl onions and parsnips. It didn't matter if morning rose before the bread did or if she fell asleep standing up; she wouldn't go to bed until every last thing was perfect.

Taming her fatigue with determination, Claire headed to the pantry and filled her arms with ingredients.

If she had to clean from dusk till dawn to keep a roof over her children's heads, food in their bellies and self-respect in their hearts, then by God she'd do it. She would muck out any stall, cook a million meals. Whatever it took. No matter what, she was going to wipe the fear and concern from Will's eyes—and keep the innocence in Orlando's and Rosalind's.

Hungry ranchers? Messy house? Filthy barn? Bring it on.

*I'm your woman, Pine Road Ranch.*

Bat dung and cobwebs. Those were the first things Fletcher Kingsley saw when he opened his eyes on...

What day was it? Thursday? Friday?

Struggling until he sat upright with his palms braced against a rough wood floor, his aching head lowered, he settled on Friday, though it didn't make much difference. The days bled together when you had nothing better to do than get drunk in your own attic.

A thin line of sweat broke out above his lip as he tried to straighten his left leg. Huge mistake. Under the best circumstances, the leg ached like a sonovabitch. Last night he'd slept with it bent against one of the several dozen dust-crusted boxes filling the low-ceilinged attic of his family home in Honeyford, Oregon. He'd climbed up here to locate a frying pan and stayed to rummage through the boxes for other homey conveniences. Except for a thirty-year-old bottle of Scotch whisky, he hadn't unearthed anything interesting, so having spent every damn day and night for the past four months in pain of one kind or another, he'd decided a shot or two of whisky couldn't hurt. Between the boredom, the boxes and the Scotch, he must have passed out. Now the pain shooting through his hip, thigh and knee was so excruciating, he almost reached for the bottle he'd set between a box labeled "Junk" and another labeled "More Junk."

*"Eeeeeeerrrrrrrrohhhhh."* A huge black-and-white cat with fur like an anemic gopher and a meow that sounded like Darth Vader hopped off the "Junk" box, slid down the cardboard side and strolled across Fletcher's crotch en route to his stomach. Yawning, the creature emitted a stream of breath that smelled like a fishing boat.

"Aw, God have mercy." Grimacing, Fletcher turned his face. The mangy feline had appeared two weeks ago, one day after his own arrival. The cat had taken one look at Fletcher, sensed a kindred spirit and stayed. Now he inched higher up on his new master's chest and forced Fletcher to deflect a lick with his hand. "You've eaten your last sardine, pal." The stubborn feline instituted a head-butting maneuver, so

Fletcher gave in and scratched a spot between the ragged ears. Immediately, a guttural purr erupted. "I *might* buy tuna."

Conversing with something live this early in the day proved exhausting. Unfortunately, just as Fletcher thought he might join his cat for another nap, the unmistakable sound of the doorbell—rigged for the past forty years to chime the Oregon state song—rang through the main level of the house. His grandfather, who had designed the bell, had possessed a good sense of humor. Fletcher did not.

Moreover, he had learned long ago that, for the good of all, some people needed to limit their contact with other living beings. He had no intention of answering the door.

Since he was in the privacy of his own empty home, he allowed himself the luxury of a deep groan. Thanks to the alcohol, his head throbbed nauseatingly to a different beat from the pain in his hip and leg. He tried breathing it down to a workable level, and the pulsing began to recede until the first bar of "Oregon, My Oregon" pealed through the house again. The idiotic thing could be heard from every cranny in the old place, like a church bell on steroids.

Employing concentrated effort, Fletcher levered himself to a stand. His head spun. As he searched for the walking stick he was certain…sort of certain…he had brought upstairs last night, the bell rang *again*, which aggravated him so much he yelled without considering the consequences, "Knock it off!" Pain seared his temples.

And the bell chimed once more.

With a grim, malevolent smile, Fletcher snatched up the bottle of whiskey and made his way toward the attic door. For two decades he'd nursed anger and resentment until the emotions had become an enduring part of him, like functioning organs, as vital as his heart and lungs. In the past he'd worked off excess steam in the rodeo ring, riding bulls and broncs with tempers as voracious as his. Four months ago he'd been injured, his rodeo days over, his restlessness and rebelliousness still intact. He'd been stewing in his own juices ever since. Damned if it wouldn't feel good to vent all over somebody else.

Limping down the steep attic stairs, his hip, leg and head pulsing with every step, he felt sorry…almost…for the chump ringing his bell.

"Orlando Dobbs, don't you dare ring that bell again!"

"It plays a song, Mommy. Listen."

"No!" Claire attempted to race up the porch steps to where her sons were standing, but she was slowed by the large, heavy basket she carried and didn't make it in time. Orlando pressed the white button for the third time, and the crazy doorbell pealed through the ranch house again. Only this time it didn't stop.

"I think it's stuck, Mom." Will looked at her solemnly.

"Oh, no." Claire set the basket of food on the weathered porch and jabbed at the white button, a vain attempt to dislodge it from where it did, indeed, seem to be stuck.

*Please let the people inside be old and deaf.*

It was possible. Pine Road Ranch looked nothing like she had originally envisioned.

The fertile land and stately home of her imagining were in fact acres of sagebrush and a house that looked as if it had been ridden hard and put away wet. Paint peeled in long strips from the wood siding, its shade an indistinct gray that might once have been blue or might once have been white. The structure of the long ranch house suggested it had long ago been graceful and welcoming, but today it sagged like a forgotten relative, weary and broken by neglect.

After a hard thud of disappointment, Claire made herself look on the bright side: help was clearly needed here.

Glancing at her sons, she hoped that bringing them along would be a boon, not a hindrance to getting the job.

She'd hustled the boys to school this morning only to be reminded that Friday was a teacher in-service day, and there were no classes. Taking her jubilant sons home, she'd dropped Rosalind off with their neighbor Irene Gould as planned, but hadn't had the heart to ask the elderly woman to take on two spirited boys as well. Neither was she willing to let any grass grow under her feet in applying for the position at Pine Road Ranch, so she'd packed Will and Orlando up along with the food.

Picking at the depressed doorbell with her fingernail while mentally pleading with it to be quiet, Claire told her sons, "I'm trying to get a job, remember? These people will expect us to be on our best behavior."

The words had barely left her mouth when a man yanked open the front door. His height and width filled the entry space. Glaring at them like Zeus defending Mount Olympus, he growled, "What the hell is going on out here?"

Instinctively, Claire gathered her sons to her side. Orlando's awestruck eyes looked huge. The last time he'd heard someone say "hell," his best friend from kindergarten had lost Berenstain Bears privileges for a week.

Angular, with many days' worth of stubble on his lean jaw, and ink-black hair that curled over his collar, the man appraised her slowly, starting at the top of her head and inching his way down. She'd donned her best outfit for the interview, a navy, scoop-necked maternity dress she'd taken in at the waist. It had seemed appropriate and professional when she'd left the house that morning. Now eyes that glinted like polished mahogany halted their study blatantly at her bosom.

The pretty speech Claire had prepared to introduce herself dissolved beneath the bold gaze, and the chilly fall morning suddenly felt like noon in July. She tugged the lapels of her coat together and picked up the basket of food.

One black brow rose ever so slightly as he noted her blush. A corner of his mouth curled.

With her heart pounding uncomfortably, Claire forced herself to speak. "Is this Pine Road Ranch?" She half hoped she'd misread the roadside sign that lead her here.

He glanced from her face to the boys to the basket over her left arm, then leaned a shoulder against the door and sighed heavily. "Let me guess: the Honeyford Ladies Society divvied up the souls to be saved this week. You drew short straw." Wicked amusement changed his eyes from hard mahogany to liquid molasses. His baritone rippled like caramel. "Darlin', here's a tip. If there's a Bible in that basket, don't pull it out. The last time I darkened the door of Honeyford Presbyterian Pastor Reed found me in the narthex trading spit with his niece."

Claire's jaw went slack, but no sound emerged from her. Orlando piped up in her stead. "Why'd you trade spit? Other people's spit has cooties. You could catch a cold that way. My mom says—"

"Are you the doorbell ringer?" the man interrupted, his black brows swooping like crows. Leaning out from the threshold, he peered at the bell. Balling his fingers into a fist, he administered one hard blow to the doorbell plate. Amazingly, the ringing stopped. He squinted at the clear sky. "Nice day. Why don't you all run along now and enjoy it somewhere else."

"Come on, Mom." Will tugged at her.

"Just a minute, sweetie." She squeezed his hand. At barely five foot three, she had to look way up to face the tall rancher, but she refused to remain cowed. "I saw a sign on the road that pointed this way for Pine Road Ranch. Did I make a mistake?"

"This is the ranch, but don't let that stop you from thinking you made a mistake. Adios."

"Wait, please—"

The door slammed on her words.

"Oh!" Stunned, Claire stood immobile for a long moment then turned to march down the porch steps. "Come on, boys."

"What'd we do?" Orlando's innocent query followed her.

Claire almost reminded him about the excessive doorbell ringing, but that nuisance did not merit such rudeness. Having grown up without common courtesy, she tried always to be polite and to instill good manners in her children. Conflict and argument were not something she courted. But when she turned to look at her sons, their pale faces and uncertain expressions made her blood boil.

"Nothing. We did absolutely nothing." It took only an instant to make a new decision. "Come on."

Marching right back to the door, she knocked. No answer, so she knocked again, harder.

With not a doubt in her mind that the man inside heard the summons and was ignoring her, Claire stood at a crossroads. Recalling his appraisal and the mocking curl of his lips when he'd assumed she was the welcome wagon, she wanted to retreat. But over her arm she carried a basket of food she'd stayed up all night to prepare, and a bad-tempered cowboy had just disrespected her in front of her boys, who had only her to turn them into men.

She glanced at the doorbell then down at Orlando, and her voice was sure and strong. "Ring it."

## Chapter Two

It took several more moments of the musical bell before the door swung open. This time the man who glared at her looked like Satan with a wedgie. "If that doorbell rings one more time, I will not be responsible for my actions."

"I knocked first," Claire responded brightly. "As I was saying, I'm here about the ad. I brought food so you'll be able to sample my cooking." She raised the heavy basket. Show and tell. "As for house cleaning, I worked weekends all last year at the Rest Up Inn, one of the finest motels in Willow Hills, Kentucky. The manager there can vouch for me. Your ad has been in the paper two days as of this morning. I'd like to get a leg up on the competition, and I'm sure you'd like to settle on an employee, so here I am."

She smiled as if she expected him to be pleased to have her here.

For what felt like a long while, he stared, his brows locked into a frown, his dark eyes expressing puzzlement but a smidge less ire than they had before. "What's your name?"

"Oh! I'm sorry." She stuck out a hand. "Claire. Claire Dobbs. We're new to town—my kids and I—and we're happy to be here and ready to make Honeyford our permanent home."

His laugh reminded her of a car that hadn't been started in a while. "Let me know how that works out for you." He did not take her hand. "Now you need to go back the way you came, Claire Dobbs. You've got the wrong place, and I'm all worn out from socializing."

Fletcher watched the line form between her pale brows. Her features were petite, narrow, and the teeth that showed when she bit her lower lip were small and well formed.

As addled by pain and the whiskey as he was, Fletcher nonetheless sensed the frantic hopefulness behind the woman's chipper self-promo.

He had no interest in fraternizing with anyone from town, and especially not with someone who kept looking at him as if he held the map to the Holy Grail.

She said she was here with her kids—no husband, which made her the kind of woman with whom he almost never traded more than a word or two. Unadorned by pretty clothes or pretty makeup or a modern hairstyle, she could have faded right off his porch, except for the spark of courage and tenacity he read in her eyes. Because she was so tiny, all that courage somehow made her seem more vulnerable.

Fletcher did not do vulnerable. He especially did not do vulnerable plus kids. He'd learned firsthand that some men were not cut out to be daddies, uncles or even brothers and that in such cases the most responsible thing was to limit all contact with people below five feet tall.

"I don't understand," she said, tilting her head like a curious bluejay. Fletcher added *cute* to her list of unwelcome qualities. "If this is Pine Road Ranch—"

*"Eeeeeerrrrrrohhhhhhh."* The cat appeared, winding around Fletcher's legs then trotting across the threshold to wind around the woman's.

"A cat!" The younger boy was instantly enthralled. "Can I pet it? What's its name?" He fell to his knees beside the shabby feline and began, with surprising gentleness, to stroke its fur. The loud purr engaged.

Fletcher scowled. "It doesn't have a name." Hesitating only a moment, he added, "And it's not mine." The cat looked up at him, its ratty ears twitching, but Fletcher refused to back down. He didn't want something that needed to be petted.

"If it doesn't have a family, can we take it? Can we?"

Fletcher shrugged.

"What?" The young woman looked between her sons and Fletcher. "No, we're not taking the cat. Boys, go on down the porch and play."

The smaller kid scooped up the cat and carried it off. The older boy left his mother's side more reluctantly.

Ms. Dobbs reached beneath a yellow cloth napkin covering the basket that hung over her forearm. "I have a clipping here from the local paper."

"Lady—"

With increasing determination, she began to read from the scrap of paper. "'Can you clean house? Muck a stall? Bake a pecan pie?—'"

"Look, I don't know what—

"Oh, no! George!" The younger kid's squeal pierced the air—and Fletcher's eardrum. "Geooooorrrrrrrrrge!" His mother and Fletcher looked up as the cat came tearing back along the porch, carrying something in its mouth, although Fletcher wasn't sure what the something was.

Skidding awkwardly to a stop, the animal assessed its

best chance of escape and decided to make a break for the sanctuary of the house.

Caught off guard and leaning heavily on his good leg, Fletcher almost lost his balance as the animal tore past him. He swore.

The woman shot him a look then turned toward her boys, who were scrambling up the steps. "What happened?"

The smaller boy was bouncing and crying so much as he tried to speak that it was impossible to understand him. The older kid said, "Orlando was showing George to the cat, and it took him."

On a sound of distress, Ms. Dobbs extended a staying hand to her sons. "Will, you stay put." Shoving the paper from which she'd been reading back into the basket, she handed the whole thing to him, instructing, "Watch your brother."

Fletcher failed to recognize her intent until she pushed past him with a quick, "Excuse me."

"What? Hey!" His head whipped between her retreating back and her children's big, mistrustful eyes. Holding up a hand, he commanded, "Stay!" as if he were speaking to beagles, not boys. When the older one pulled his brother close and glared, Fletcher modified the stop-sign gesture into a one-finger warning. "Don't move. Your mother is coming right out."

A tear the size of a small marble rolled down the younger kid's cheek. His mouth wobbled and pathetic hiccups punctuated his question, "Can you get George back?"

Tension pinched deep inside Fletcher's chest and fueled the craving for a roll of antacids. *Damn, damn, damn.*

*This* was why he didn't want people on his ranch, or around him at all. People made peace impossible.

Turning without making a promise about anything, he left the door ajar and limped as quickly as he could toward his living room. She was there, facing down the dog-sized cat, which had its belly on the ground, the thing in its mouth and a low growl emanating from deep inside.

"Come on, kitty, I need George back." She spoke low and persuasively. Bending from the waist, she reached out a hand as she advanced on the animal. "Come on. Drop him now."

"Don't touch that cat!" Fletcher's strong warning made her jump. "I don't know anything about it. It could get mean."

Claire looked at him in consternation. "I have to get George back."

"What is George?"

"Orlando's mouse."

"A mouse?" *Sweet Jesus.* The cat was a compulsive eater. George was hamburger.

Picturing the tears and trauma when the kid discovered his mouse had been eaten, Fletcher decided once again that as soon as he cleared everyone out of here, there would be no more people, no more cats, no more mice in his home. Correction—this wasn't even his home yet, though it should have been. The deed to the ranch would only become his upon fulfillment of a stipulation in his father's will—an insane, archaic stipulation that fed Fletcher's rage every time he thought about it. And which he had no intention of fulfilling.

Fletcher's relationship with his father was just one of the reasons he preferred solitude today. He'd had enough of other people's expectations to last a lifetime. Once he got the will straightened out and Pine Road Ranch put in his name, he intended to have animals *in the barn,* a foreman and maybe a couple of hands—all of whom could find their own, off-ranch housing.

Crossing to the fireplace, he reached for a thick coil of rope that was hanging on a hook. His favorite lasso. He hadn't used it since last summer, prior to the accident and his retirement from rodeo.

Carefully gauging his distance from the cat and the length

of rope he would need, Fletcher lifted a finger to his lips to instruct Claire to remain silent. He took a couple of steps toward the husky feline, raised the rope and began to swirl it rhythmically over his head. The cat did not seem intimidated in the least until Fletcher stamped his foot hard on the wood floor. Startled then, the cat leaped up, and Fletcher threw his rope.

Thank God the creature didn't fight, beyond one of its alien-sounding meows. The mouse dropped to the ground and lay still, and the cat, instead of struggling, crouched its big body down to the floor, rolled over and began to play with the rope around its middle.

Fletcher moved as quickly as he could to release the cat. The mouse, he figured, was a goner, but the woman said, "Thank you *so* much! Oh, my goodness, that was such a surprise. For a second, I thought my heart stopped."

She stepped forward to retrieve the mouse as Fletcher was removing the rope from the cat, and their arms brushed. He smelled something clean and feminine, like lemon and flowers. The scent went straight to his head, clearing it for an instant, making him recall just briefly what it was like to think about soft skin and sweet lips and nothing more serious than where to make love. No moment had been that simple in months.

Pushing himself to a stand, he struggled when his left leg and hip refused to cooperate. Unfortunately, he'd set his walking stick aside when he'd picked up the lasso. A slim hand immediately grasped his elbow to help him up.

"Oops! I've got you."

She had him? He outweighed her by a good seventy pounds.

"Is that your cane?" She nodded to the brick hearth. "You stay put. I'll get it."

"No—" But she was already moving.

Spry and brisk, like a no-nonsense fairy, she fetched the fancy carved walking stick, handed it to him with care and then seemed to be waiting to make sure he was steady.

An unfamiliar cocktail of gratitude and humiliation flowed in his veins.

When he was in the hospital last summer, a girl had visited him, a barrel racer with whom he slept if they happened to be in the same city. They'd been together the night before the accident, so she'd stopped by before she left town. She'd eaten the Jell-O off his lunch tray, had written something risqué on his cast and told him she was heading to Spain that afternoon for the Rodeo Europe Tour. She hadn't asked if he needed a drink of water or a back scratch or how he planned to get along when they let him out of the hospital. She hadn't promised to call. He hadn't expected her to.

He hadn't felt the least bit irritated with her.

"Where's the mouse?" he asked around the dryness in his mouth.

"Oh, it's right here." Claire Dobbs patted a pocket on the front of her dress and smiled. "Safe and sound. Thank heavens."

Safe and sound? "It's not dead?"

She laughed, a tinkling sound that made her seem younger and happier. "No more than before. Orlando's been carrying that old mouse in his pocket going on two years now. I wash it when I can get it away from him."

"You bathe the mouse?"

Pulling it from her pocket, she held it up for examination. "It doesn't look too much worse for the wear. I don't think your cat hurt it any."

On her palm rested a furry, dark gray, *stuffed* mouse.

"It's a toy." Fletcher stared at it in disbelief. "I lassoed a cat for a toy?"

She looked up at him, her light hazel eyes larger and their

expression more open than before. "I truly appreciate that. Orlando's daddy gave him the mouse when our landlord said we couldn't have real pets. My husband passed on shortly after that. George was his last gift to our son."

A widow.

"How long ago was that?" The words escaped the lock he usually kept on his lips, and he wanted to kick his own ass.

"It'll be a year in three weeks." The sentence cracked in the middle, but she completed it and pressed her lips together. Devoid of self-pity, her smile held an aching sweetness.

Fletcher felt a stabbing pain beneath his ribs. He knew about grief, knew how to feel it and how to bury it. What he did not know was how to respond to it, and he didn't intend to try.

"Okay." Gesturing toward the toy, he hoped she'd take the hint. "You've got it back now, so—"

"We got scared out there alone."

The older kid appeared at the entry to the living room, holding his brother by one hand and hauling the large picnic basket in the other. He didn't look scared; rather, his lowered brow and tight jaw made him look like a small bouncer.

Fletcher dragged a hand down his face. He didn't know how he had wound up with a widow and two kids in a house he'd planned to bar against all visitors, but it was going to end *now*.

"All right." He used his best *this is final* voice. "So we're done here—"

"Did he give you a job?" The older boy spoke up again, addressing his mother. Then he turned his attention to Fletcher, and the belligerence was plain in his voice and expression as he raised the picnic basket. "Our mom made all this food for you. Aren't you gonna taste it?"

"Will," his mother remonstrated gently.

"You did!" Glaring at Fletcher, Will accused, "She made

all this stuff. You didn't even look at all the stuff she made for you."

"You should at least take a no-thank-you bite," Orlando, the smaller boy instructed.

"Orlie." Claire spoke kindly but firmly.

"You make us take 'em. I had to eat bruss's spouts. That's way worse than what he's gotta taste."

Claire moved to her sons. She trailed her fingers gently down Orlando's cheek then rested a hand on Will's shoulder. Relieving him of the heavy basket, she faced Fletcher. From sweet and open, her gaze returned to wary and protective, and he felt that damned unwelcome pinch of guilt.

"You told me this wasn't the right place, but the plaque over your mantel says 'Pine Road Ranch.' If you've already hired someone or you didn't think I was right for the position, you could have said so." She colored slightly. "Oh. I guess you were trying to tell me that." Her chin lifted. "I apologize. We'll leave you alone now. Come on, boys." Hefting the heavy picnic basket, she took her younger son's hand.

Fletcher should have left well enough alone, but her apology irked a hell of a lot more than her anger would have.

"I am not hiring anyone. And what the hell would a picnic have to do with it?"

Orlando giggled. The reason was a mystery to Fletcher until Claire Dobbs warned tightly, "Mister, you are standing before impressionable children. *Stop swearing.*"

Releasing Orlando's hand, she again reached into the basket to withdraw the piece of newsprint. This time, instead of reading aloud, she handed it to Fletcher. "This was in *The Buzz* yesterday. It's got the name of your ranch. And your address is right there at the end."

Fletcher frowned. Squinting, he scanned the clipping.

*Two years' guaranteed employment for an honest, hard-*

*working woman. Can you clean house, muck a stall, bake
a pecan pie?*

What the hell...heck.

*Integrity and loyalty a must to join the team at Pine Road
Ranch.*

Team?

*Apply in person. 120056 Old Pine Road. Benefits.*

"I didn't write this."

"Then somebody else here—" the woman began, but
Fletcher relieved her of that idea immediately.

"There isn't anyone else. I'm 'the team.'" And that was
his address, and the name of the ranch.

And he loved pecan pie.

Suspicion began to edge out surprise. Only someone familiar with the terms of his father's will could have placed
the ad.

Plowing a hand through his hair, Fletcher rubbed his aching skull. He'd been avoiding his brother since he'd arrived
in Honeyford. It was time to go toe-to-toe with Dean about
the damned will—and about the employment notice if Dean
had anything to do with it.

"So the address is a mistake." With her delicate brows
drawn together, Claire Dobbs tried once again to understand.
"Is there another ranch on this road?" Renewed hope, as
palpable as it was sudden, lit her face.

Fletcher felt his gut knot.

*Two years of guaranteed employment...*

*Join the team at Pine Road Ranch...*

The urge to throw something came on strongly as suspicion grew. His father's will had been clear: marry or forfeit
the ranch. Most of Honeyford knew that he had routinely done
the opposite of anything his father had told him to do. Someone who knew about the marriage codicil and who wanted to
yank Fletcher's chain had put that ad in the paper. Given his

misspent youth, there had to be plenty of people in Honeyford who would love to stick it to him—there was no love lost between him and this town—but Fletcher doubted that many knew about the will. That narrowed the field considerably.

"Maybe someone at the paper mistook the locations," she concluded. "Do you know of anyone nearby who's hiring?"

For the first time, he noticed that the woman's dress wasn't merely dowdy; the material was cheap and the fit ill, though it hugged her breasts better than any other part of her. Still, the garment belonged on a thrift-store discount rack, not on her. He glanced at her sons and saw that their jackets were worn, clearly hand-me-downs that had lived through more than a few winters.

A burning sensation crawled through Fletcher's veins. When he found exactly who wrote that asinine ad, he was going to kick some wiseacre ass.

"There wasn't a mistake," he told her. "The ad was referring to this ranch, but it sounds as if I'm hiring a housekeeper, and I definitely am not. This—" he held up the scrap of paper "—is a sort of…joke. There's no job."

"A joke." Her brows inched toward her hairline. "You mean…a funny joke?"

Pressing his thumb and forefinger against his eyelids, Fletcher reminded himself that this was neither his fault nor his responsibility. He didn't want to get into it any further. "Sorry," was all he added.

Claire Dobbs's eyes grew so wide he could see white all around the irises. "You put a 'help-wanted' notice in a community paper as a joke?"

"Me? No—"

"In this economy? What planet are you living on?" She went from kind to outraged in seconds. "That was the first job notice I've seen since we moved here. People need hope and security right now, not…someone's warped idea of funny!"

Her cheeks were red, her eyes bright and glassy. Fletcher sincerely hoped she was not about to cry, because if there was anything he hated more than his own emotions, it was somebody else's.

But she didn't cry, and she didn't back off. Her Southern accent, which had previously softened her words, now sharply underscored her fury.

"Have you got any idea how badly I wanted this? Or how hard I worked to get ready for this interview?" The finger she pointed shook. "And you're 'sorry'? Well, I should say you're sorry. Mister, you are one sorry excuse for a human being!"

She turned toward her sons, who looked as if they had never seen their mother so angry. "We're done here."

The older boy, Will, flanked her protectively, a pup doing the job of a guard dog.

Orlando asked, "Aren't we gonna work here?"

"No," she said, her voice low, choked. Her chin, however, remained high; her gaze straight ahead and stoic as she started to leave.

"I thought he was gonna eat the food you brang and then we could have the leftovers," the younger boy protested. "Can I have a cinnamon bun? I ate all my oatmeal this morning, and—"

"Cut it out, Orlie," Will ordered, glaring at Fletcher. "Do what you're told."

"You're not the boss of me."

"Mom is."

"Okay," Orlando mumbled, looking disappointed and confused. "Where's George?"

As furious as she was, Claire mustered a reassuring smile. "In my pocket."

She left then, without a backward glance, but Will looked over his shoulder on the way out of the room. As if wishing his eyes held superpowers, he leveled Fletcher with a gaze meant to sear.

Fletcher watched their retreating backs, battling the guilt he loathed.

He tried to stay away from people—didn't he try?—and he attempted to make people stay away from him. *Don't ask, don't offer*—that was his policy, yet here he was, feeling as if he'd yanked the wings off a butterfly.

*"Eeeeeeeorrrrrrrooooowwwww."* The cat padded to him across the old, carpeted floor, apparently willing to forgive and forget the lasso. It blinked up at Fletcher, looking ready for a nap now that its toy had been confiscated.

"Get out," Fletcher told it flatly.

The giant tomcat sat, licked its hind leg and purred.

Fletcher brought the walking stick down heavily as he limped from the room.

Freedom had been his goal when he'd left Honeyford ten years ago; it was his goal still. Freedom from the people, places and situations that made peace impossible.

There wasn't a snowball's chance that he'd take a wife, not even to secure the ranch. Be someone's husband? He laughed with no humor at all. Yeah, that was bound to be a success.

Honeyford was filled with ghosts from his past, and he was going to get rid of them, once and for all. He had plans—plans involving land, horses and vengeance, not women, children, overweight cats, or, God forbid, marriage.

"Don't get comfortable," he told the complacent tom on his way to the bathroom. "I don't want a cat."

He didn't—he honest-to-God didn't—want anything.


Thriving horse and sheep ranches had once surrounded Honeyford, Oregon, population 1,812. The larger operations had sold out over the years as recent generations headed to college and to bigger towns with more opportunity. Now

Honeyford functioned primarily as a bedroom community to the vital city of Bend, some eighty miles west.

Honeyford's first settlers had been a family of beekeepers named Castrignano. Only one of their descendents remained in the area and rumor had it she was terrified of bees, but the businesses in town still bore names like Honey Bea's Bakery, Delilah's Hair Hive, the Honey Pot Café, Drone Hardware and *The Buzz*. The latter was the local throwaway paper from which Claire had clipped the unexplained ad.

At nine twenty-five on Friday, Fletcher parked his pickup in front of King's Pharmacy, one of the few businesses whose moniker made no reference to anything bee or honey related. The pharmacy's hours were ten-to-six on Fridays. Fletcher purposely arrived a half hour before opening.

Bypassing the entrance, he walked around the corner and through the alley until he arrived at the back of the old brick building. Painstakingly, he made his way up a steep flight of wooden steps that led to a second-floor apartment.

Though the day was clear and chilly, sweat beaded Fletcher's brow as he rang the bell and waited for the door to open. The memory of one particular visit to this apartment remained fresh and raw nearly twenty years after the fact. That time, his father had been on the other side of the threshold and Fletcher had been an eight-year-old boy about to learn that the world could be an ugly place. Fletcher had detested coming to the apartment, to the pharmacy, even to Honeyford itself from that day forward.

Today the apartment belonged to Dean, Fletcher's half brother, who was also the pharmacist in residence downstairs.

When the door opened, Fletcher was glad to have the element of surprise on his side.

He had dressed for this reunion in dark jeans, a black leather jacket and black boots. His beard was two days old, his hair about a month overdue for a trim. By contrast, his big brother looked as much like a choirboy as he had the day he'd given his high school valedictory address. At thirty-five, Dean had lines around his mouth and on his forehead, but his hair remained a rich brown, several shades lighter than Fletcher's and combed with a neat side part. Even his lab coat was whiter than new snow and perfectly pressed.

Fletcher leaned a shoulder against the doorjamb and sent his gaze roving slowly over the brother he had seen only twice in the past five years. He allowed a small smile to play about his lips. Then he whistled. "Lookit you. How do you get your whites so bright?"

For a time, Dean stared back without speaking. Then he remembered his manners, stepped aside and gestured for Fletcher to enter. "Come in." He shook his head as if to clear it. "You caught me by surprise. I expected you to ignore me until I came to you."

Fletcher released a bark of laughter. "Still as honest as Abe."

"It wasn't an insult." Dean's already stick-straight spine stiffened. "I'd heard you moved into the ranch, and—"

"I'm hardly offended." Fletcher waved the explanation away. "We both know if it weren't for the will, I wouldn't have stepped foot in this place."

Relying heavily on his walking stick, Fletcher entered and looked around. Dean had put his own stamp on the apartment, with a traditional sofa in brown leather, a burgundy chair and a reasonable number of technological luxuries. The whole place was neat as a pin.

"I've got a pot of coffee on, if you don't mind it strong." Observant gray eyes followed Fletcher's progress into the room then came to rest on the cane. Dean's brows lowered. "What happened?"

"A stallion named Negro Muerte and I had a bet going.

We'd been trying for a year to see who'd break first. He won."

When his brother's full lips pursed with worry, Fletcher grimaced. He had never minded the presence of a stadium full of strangers watching while a bull tossed him into the air like a Beanie Baby, but he'd crawl out of his skin if he thought Dean felt sorry for him.

"How about a beer?" he suggested, though the mere thought of alcohol turned his stomach. Still, incurring his brother's disapproval had always been easier than incurring Dean's empathy, and it seemed the old tricks still worked.

"It's 9:30 a.m."

Moving toward the sofa, he cracked, "It'll be happy hour by the time I sit down." He halted, affecting a frown. "Ah, you know what? Never mind the beverage. You're busy, I'm busy. Let's get right to the point: I want the title to Pine Road Ranch. Today. I'm not going to be manipulated in some posthumous attempt by Victor to bring me into line. Or whatever he thought he was doing when he wrote up that will. And if you helped him—"

Dean held up a hand. "Hold on—"

"—then you're going to get to know my lawyer really well—"

"Hey! Shut up for a minute!" Lips compressed and head wagging, Dean regarded his brother with resignation. "Welcome home."

## Chapter Three

Crossing to the burgundy wing chair by the window, Dean dropped into it and stared up at his younger brother. "When Dad's attorney phoned, I take it he read only the part of the will that pertains to you?"

"He read the part that says I have to get married and stay that way two years or the ranch will be forfeited. I hung up after that."

"You hung up him?" Dean shook his head. "So you don't know the rest of the terms? What happens to the ranch if you default?"

"I assume you get it."

"Me? No! Dad would have realized I'd sign the ranch right back to you. And I'm sure he didn't want to add more strain to our relationship. He always hoped we'd..." Sighing, Dean gazed out the window that overlooked the alley behind the pharmacy. "Whatever you think of him, Dad had strong family values."

In his head, Fletcher made a very rude comment. Outwardly, he indulged in only a slight raise of his brows. Dean was Victor's first son, from a first marriage that, as far as Fletcher could see, hadn't lasted long enough to turn sour. Dean's early memories of family life were good.

Though Fletcher had hated their father with a passion bordering on rabid, and though he had never made a secret of it, he had nonetheless kept the worst truths about Victor to himself. At times he had felt like a garbage can, collecting all the waste so the room's other occupants could live trash free.

Dean liked to believe he lived in a Beaver Cleaver world. Let him.

Hoping to get the meeting over with, Fletcher said, "I assume you attended the reading of the will."

"Of course."

"Fine, then lay it on me. If you don't get the ranch, who does?"

"The city."

"The city." Fletcher took two steps toward his brother, bringing his cane down hard with each step. "I lose a ranch that was in my mother's family—not Victor's—for three generations unless I get married and stay that way for two years? And if I default, the land belongs to Honeyford?" The town Victor knew both his younger son and his late second wife had hated, for a buffet of reasons.

"Yes."

The impulse to hurl his walking stick through the window above Dean's head came on strongly. Fletcher controlled it with effort. "I planned to make you sell the ranch back to me. Now what?"

Dean shrugged. "Let it go to the city and then try to buy it back. Or get married."

Fletcher glared, his gaze narrowing suspiciously. "About that ad in *The Buzz*—"

"Get any responses yet?" Dean's smile curled one side of his mouth. "It seemed atypical of you, but I have to admit, it's not a terrible way to meet women, assuming you can screen them well over the phone."

"What?" Fletcher's brow lowered skeptically. He wasn't sure whether to believe what he was hearing. "You think *I* placed that ad?"

"Who else?"

"You."

"Me?"

Dean's surprise was so genuine, Fletcher forced himself to accept that he was barking up the wrong tree. "Or Lanford Morgan," he tried. "Is he still the editor of *The Buzz*?"

"Yeah. But why would Lanny put that in the paper without your knowledge?"

Fletcher paused briefly then snapped, "As a joke."

"A joke?" Dean repeated doubtfully. "Lanny?"

The truth, even all these years later, was not pretty. Dean had been in college by the time Lanford and Fletcher had entered high school, so he'd missed some of his brother's most obnoxious moments.

With golden-boy Deano away earning a higher education, straight-arrow Lanny had assumed Dean's after-school job at the pharmacy and had, as far as Victor Kingsley was concerned, become the new standard of excellence against which Fletcher was measured. Furious at his father, but powerless to change his circumstances, Fletcher had paid Lanford back several times over for making his relationship with Victor even more miserable than it had previously been.

"It was probably a practical joke," Fletcher explained. "For revenge."

"What did you do to him?"

*Among other things?* "Smeared honey in his jock strap before gym."

Rubbing his brow, Dean shook his head. Though he was only thirty-five, and single, he'd already mastered his *Father Knows-Best* smile. "Well, I'm sure Lanny owes you, and it's true he wasn't exactly overjoyed to hear you'd come home, but I don't think he wrote the ad. He showed it to me earlier in the week. It arrived at his office with a cashier's check and typewritten instructions, but no signature and no return address. He assumed you sent it."

Fletcher believed Dean, which raised another suspicion. "How many people know about the will?"

An attack of conscience showed plainly on Dean's handsome, clean-cut face. "I discussed a couple of the details with Lanny."

Fletcher swore. "Lanford Morgan has always had the biggest mouth this side of the Cascades. Now I'll have to kill him." Turning, he headed for the door.

"Hey! Don't you want to know what the will states for me?" Dean called after him.

"You got the pharmacy, the building we're standing in and a gold cup engraved 'Son of the Year.'"

"Not quite." Dean stood and spoke before his brother could leave. "Dad made getting married a prerequisite to your inheriting the ranch *and* to my inheriting this building. The pharmacy—the business alone—is mine, but to own the building in which I work and live, I need to get and stay married to a 'decent' woman. Same as you."

Taking his hand from the doorknob, Fletcher executed an awkward pivot. "I don't believe it. He screwed you over too?"

Dean expelled a long, slow breath. "I feel manipulated, yes. But we're not being screwed over. I already know you're no going to believe this so you can withhold the profanities, but I believe that misguided or not, Dad is trying to save us."

"Victor—" Fletcher refused to say Dad "—is trying to save us." As requested, he swallowed the epithet that rose to mind, but his cynicism was ripe. "From what?"

In the clean morning light, Dean smiled sadly. "Ourselves."

By the time the men's reunion was over, Fletcher's head felt like a basketball being dribbled, so he followed Dean down the stairs leading into King's Pharmacy and went in search of ibuprofen.

The brothers had long ago claimed their roles in the family drama. Dean was the mediator, a regular Pollyanna who made honey out of horse manure. The spin he put on the will diluted Victor to a harmless eccentric afraid his sons would end up lonely unless he goaded them into marriage.

Fletcher, on the other hand, had learned two decades ago that their father didn't give a damn about anyone but himself. No one came between Victor Kingsley and his personal agenda. What that agenda was this time, Fletcher couldn't be certain, but he knew one thing: Victor had hated Pine Road Ranch almost as much as Fletcher and his mother had loved it.

The elder Kingsley had been a doctor, not a cowboy like the younger son with whom he had continually fought. Victor had felt distaste for anything he couldn't control—the land, his young wife, his second son.

Pine Road Ranch had been in Fletcher's mother's family to begin with and should never have belonged to Victor, who had turned it over to lackadaisical renters.

Over the past several years, as rodeo championships and commercial endorsements feathered Fletcher's bank account, he had tried via lawyers to purchase the property, offering far more than it was worth. The answer from his father had been a flat no every time.

Choosing a painkiller and ferrying it to the pharmacy cash register at the rear of the store, Fletcher felt one hundred percent committed to staying at the ranch, no matter what. He'd broken a window to gain entrance the day he'd arrived. Moving his stuff in, he'd changed every lock then informed Victor's lawyer by e-mail that he intended to stay put. So far, he hadn't heard from anyone who wanted to evict him.

Dean was ringing up a customer and counseling her when Fletcher approached the register. "This needs to be taken with food, but it can be something small, a few bites of cereal or an arrowroot biscuit. We stock a good one made with molasses." He winked. "Remember the advice about a spoonful of sugar."

Holy cow. His brother had turned into a hybrid of Marcus Welby and Mary Poppins. No wonder he wasn't outraged over being coerced into marriage. Dean was born to nurture.

Distracting himself while he waited behind the woman, whose cap-covered head nodded attentively while Dean spoke, Fletcher glanced at the wide variety of donation containers atop the counter. Pictures and notes, some typed and some handwritten, were taped to the fronts of canisters and jars with slits cut in all the lids, inviting folks to donate to a medical fund for Lindy Hooper, who'd broken her hip on a senior bus tour, and to give heartily to causes like Honeyford for the Holidays, which attempted to lure tourists by dressing the locals in Victorian costumes and handing out hot cider and chestnuts. Other containers lobbied for donations for causes too irrelevant to even consider. Fletcher shook his head. Apparently his brother couldn't say no.

He tried to catch Dean's eye so he could give the signal to wrap it up, but Dean wasn't looking. "You should notice significant suppression of her cough by this afternoon. If not, give me a call here or on my cell. I wrote the number on the bottle."

He handed the woman her change, which she carefully divided among three of the containers. Dean bestowed a smile that doubtlessly made every single female heart in Honeyford fibrillate. "Thank you, Claire. I know that will be appreciated."

Fletcher found his own hand diving automatically into his pocket for coins, but he pulled it out. He did not require his brother's sugarcoated approval.

Expecting the woman in front to take her bag and go, he almost bumped into her back when she hesitated.

"Mr. Kingsley—"

"Dean."

"Thank you. Dean. I was wondering if you ever need any help here?" Her upbeat tone sounded forced, the words wrapped in meringue-soft sweetness and a southern accent. *Oh, no.* "I'm looking for a job, and if you have anything...I mean, not working with medicines, of course, but if you need someone to make deliveries or to stock shelves or clean up?" She ended hopefully.

An invisible fist socked Fletcher right in the gut. There was no mistaking that voice, a combination of sleepy South and crisp good manners...when she wasn't furious. The woman's knit cap covered hair Fletcher remembered as having the color of a wheat field, and her large trench coat covered most of the rest of her, but he was certain: the woman in front of him was the woman who had rung his doorbell early this morning.

He experienced an uncharacteristic desire to run away.

Dean's expression grew concerned as he listened to her inquiry—more of an entreaty, really. Fletcher could see the struggle inside his brother and the sincere regret when he told her, "I haven't got anything right now, Claire. But there's a bulletin board at the front of the store, and occasionally—"

"I already checked. That's all right. Times are hard for everyone. Thank you." She turned away from Dean.

Fletcher's leg wouldn't allow him to move quickly, but he reared back as if a truck rather than one petite woman were bearing down on him. And then he saw it.

*Aw, man.* Under her big, shapeless coat, a baby slept in a crisscross of material that held it to its mother's body. He saw a head of sandy ringlets and a small hand clutching its mother's shirt in sleep. She had a baby. In addition to the two boys she'd brought with her to his house.

Deep in thought, she wasn't looking at him, and he could have escaped undetected if he hadn't impulsively blurted, "Hello."

The woman looked up. It took a moment for recognition to set in. When it did, her expression changed from pensive to downright troubled.

"Where are your boys?" he asked, then grimaced. One of her sons had been on the verge of tears when he'd left this morning and the other had looked as if he'd like to see Fletcher hanging from a tree.

"The boys are at the soda fountain," she murmured then nibbled on her lower lip, worry puckering her otherwise seamless brow.

Fletcher realized she was younger than he'd originally assumed. Fatigue made her naturally fair skin seem wan, plus it put shadows beneath eyes that were actually a pretty greenish-gray color when viewed up close. Earlier this morning, he'd figured her to be at least thirty; now he revised that number down to…twenty-six? Twenty-seven?

Looking more closely at the baby wrapped against her, Fletcher saw that its teeny nose was a snot faucet. He couldn't imagine wanting even one miniature human, much less three.

Remembering that her husband had passed, he put two and two together and felt guilt again, like heartburn that wouldn't leave. She was looking for work; presumably that made her the sole support of three kids, one of which couldn't do anything more useful than sneeze and drool.

*Not your responsibility. Not remotely.*

Putting his hand in his pocket, he withdrew his wallet to pay for the ibuprofen. Since he was never a big fan of conversation anyway, he decided on a final nod only, before heading up to the register.

She, however, had more to say. Rubbing comforting circles on the baby's back, she told Fletcher, "I'm glad we ran into each other like this. I was planning to come by your place again later, anyway, to apologize."

Apologize? Fletcher wondered if he'd heard her correctly, or if she'd said she planned to drop by to demand the apology he still hadn't delivered decently.

When Victor Kingsley was alive, he had tried for nearly two decades to instill a sense of decency in his younger son. Fletcher remembered the lessons as a hot, bitter sensation that seeped through the blood and soured the mouth like medicine. Now when he tried to apologize—which wasn't often—he felt as if he were trying to speak around shards of glass. Just one of many reasons why it was easier *not to get involved.*

Claire Dobbs lifted her chin. Her expression assumed an almost exaggerated air of honor. "I apologize for yelling at you before. I may not understand your humor, but that's no excuse for disrespecting you in your own home. And especially not in front of my children. I try to set a better example than that."

Fletcher closed his eyes briefly. He was going to hell, no doubt about it.

"You set a fine example." By "humor," he assumed she

meant the fake ad. But he'd given her plenty of other reasons to disrespect him, and he knew it.

"My boys want to apologize to you, too."

*I bet.*

"They're just up at the front if you have a minute right now, Mr.—" She shook her head. "I'm sorry, I don't know your name."

Dean had been observing silently, but with keen interest. Now he waded in. "This is a surprise. I didn't know you'd met my brother."

"Brother?" Her index finger stabbed the air between them. "You're brothers?"

Her shock might have been amusing had Fletcher not spent almost three decades on the wrong side of that comparison.

"Half brothers," he supplied tersely.

"Fletcher's been away awhile. I'm hoping we'll be able to keep him home now." Dean sounded sincere. "How did you two meet?"

Fletcher managed to stifle a groan, but just barely. He had now officially exceeded his yearly quota of socializing.

He raised the bottle of ibuprofen. "Put this on my tab."

"You don't have a tab."

Growling through his teeth, he ordered, "Start one." He looked down at the woman. "Your boys were defending you. Don't make them apologize. I deserved a helluva lot worse."

With a smile more feral than fraternal, he nodded to his brother, slipped the bottle of pills into his jacket pocket and headed toward the front of the store. Behind him, he heard Dean say something to Claire, but after years of trying to hear everything going on behind closed doors, he had become equally adept at filtering out other people's conversations.

Using the walking stick, he propelled himself through

the drugstore as quickly as he could, eager to get outside. As a kid, he'd had to work here, just like Dean, and he'd hated it. The eighty-year-old building held some of his worst memories.

He had almost reached the entrance when he heard a high voice say, "I'm going to have two chocolates and one strawberry with marshmallows and sprinkles and these."

The smart thing, of course, would have been to continue walking until he was standing on the sidewalk, the string of bells jingling against the glass door behind him.

Behaving instead as if he didn't have the sense God gave a lemming, Fletcher turned toward the antique soda fountain, and there, on a shiny patent-leather stool, perched a small boy with curly blond hair. He pointed enthusiastically to a gallon jar of chocolate-covered malt balls, the candy that Fletcher, too, had loved to dump on his ice cream when he was a kid.

Orlando.

"I want vanilla with chocolate sauce and those." William sat on a stool beside his brother, his thin frame curved into a *C* as he stated his preference. He pointed to a jar of Butterfinger bars broken into bite-sized bits.

"How many scoops?" Orlando asked, his gaze on the goods.

"Hmm." William frowned as he thought. "Maybe we can afford…one each."

"One? But I want chocolate and strawberry."

"We have to save enough so we can buy one for Mom and Rozzy."

"But this is for pretend. I can get three scoops if it's pretend."

Pretend? Fletcher frowned. They were practically salivating. Growing up, he and Dean had been able to stop by the pharmacy for a double dip anytime.

"Boys. We're ready to go."

Their mother, Claire, walked up, the baby still asleep against her chest. She smiled tiredly at her sons, unaware of Fletcher standing near the entrance.

Orlando swiveled on his stool. "Mom? If we got one scoop each, could we—"

She began shaking her head apologetically before he finished. "I have cookies at home for after supper."

After supper? It wasn't even lunch yet. That was a long wait. Fletcher looked at the boys and knew they were thinking the same thing, but rather than begging, her children complied. William slid off the stool, resigned in a way Fletcher thought no boy his age ought to be, and Orlando stared longingly at the candy jars. Fletcher recalled their mother carefully counting out change for the donation canisters.

*Leave. Right now,* he thought.

"Let's go, guys."

Orlando reached out to touch the jar with the malt balls, as if to say, *See you later,* before he, too, slid off the stool.

*Go now.*

Unfortunately, Fletcher proved once again that he was a failure at following sound advice, even when he gave it to himself.

"You're not leaving yet, are you? It's Free Friday." When he spoke, both boys turned huge, wary eyes on him. The woman's gaze jerked toward his, and instinctively she put a protective hand on her daughter. The small family appeared frozen, staring at him as if he were public enemy number one.

"Free Friday," he stated again, clearing his throat when his voice sounded gruff. "One scoop, one topping, any flavor. For free. Didn't you see the sign?"

Orlando was the first to defrost. Hope and anticipation limed his expression. "We can't read yet."

William smacked the back of his hand against his brother's shoulder. "I can."

"So can I," said their mother.

He met her eyes. Suspicion lurked in the lake-like hazel, as if she was willing to see where he was headed, but ready to jump in at a moment's notice. She'd barely reach his chin if they were standing face-to-face, but Fletcher could tell simply by looking at her that she'd filet anyone who dared hurt her babies.

He wondered how long her husband had been gone.

The woman seemed perpetually on guard and damned tired. At first glance, her fair skin, eyes and hair formed an almost monochromatic palette. The women he spent time with were primary colors, bold and loud. The female before him was a pastel.

He had visited an art museum once in Chicago, going alone on a whim and joining a tour that had introduced him to Seurat, Cezanne and Monet. He'd thought at the time that an ignoramus like him would have walked right past those paintings if it hadn't been for the docent leading the tour. This woman, Claire, reminded him of the Monets; the closer he looked, the more shades he could see. And he saw that she knew he was making this up as he went along.

"Dean!" he called loudly to the back of the store. "Customers at the fountain!" When his brother arrived, Fletcher said, "I told them about Free Friday. One scoop, one topping. No charge." He nodded. "See you."

"Whoa!" Dean's hand shot out. "Free Friday?" He raised a brow and shook his head. "I'm shy one staff member today, Fletcher. Lea Simmons is down with the flu, so I'm not prepared for…Free Friday." Crossing his arms over his white lab coat, he smiled. "On the other hand, I bet you remember how to man the fountain. Everything's the same. Have at it." Before Fletcher could refuse, Dean strode off, loafers squeaking on the clean floor. "Use a bar towel to wipe up when you're through," he called before disappearing down the cold remedies aisle.

Orlando looked at Fletcher expectantly, William eyeballed him with reservation but interest and Claire's expression changed slowly from suspicion to curiosity. When she raised a fair eyebrow, he saw the challenge in her gaze.

Fletcher's jaw locked. He had particularly loathed working the ice cream counter in his youth. Dean knew that. He didn't expect to enjoy it any better right now. But Claire was looking at him, gauging whether he was going to step up to the plate or disappoint her kids.

Once he'd stationed himself behind the old-fashioned marble slab and the jars of dry toppings, he looked at his customers. It had been a long, long time since he'd tried to change anyone's opinion of him.

*And I'm not trying to now,* he told himself. He was simply…assuaging his guilt. He'd been hung over when the woman arrived at his door. And, he'd made Will believe he had to defend his family from a grown man. Fletcher knew that feeling.

Dishing up a couple of sundaes by way of apology wasn't much, but it was probably the best he could do.

Grasping the flat ice-cream scoop, heavy and familiar in his hand even after all these years, he nodded to the smaller boy first, the one who wanted three scoops and a zillion toppings.

"What'll it be?"

He caught Claire looking at him as he reached into the ice cream case. Warm and steady, her eyes conveyed appreciation, pure and unstinting, miraculously free of the judgment he knew he still deserved.

For a moment, he felt strange, ungrounded, as if he were

falling. When she started to smile—the gentlest curve of un-glossed lips—his throat constricted.

Looking away, he shoveled the ice cream scoop forcefully into the chocolate.

Dean's food costs were about to go way up.

## Chapter Four

Claire swayed gently, rocking her sleeping daughter as she watched the tall, stern man behind the counter assemble sundaes for her sons.

The rude, inhospitable rancher she'd met this morning was kind Dean Kingsley's half brother. That alone had come as a huge surprise. Then, as forbidding as he had seemed earlier, he'd gone and made up a story about free ice cream just so her kids wouldn't have to do without. The man was a mystery, for sure.

Men in general had never fit easily into Claire's comfort zone; she liked to keep the ones like Fletcher—big, masculine and imposing—at a safe distance. When she'd been a young teenager, her own mother had told her she was too school-marmish to attract a "real man." That had been fine by Claire. She'd met Arlo, her gentle and respectful Arlo, at fifteen and had known right away he was the one for her. She'd felt relief and peace in his company. A man like Fletcher Kingsley tended to give a woman like her the heebie-jeebies. He was too...masculine.

He'd taken off his jacket before he'd gotten down to work, and Claire realized that the flex of his shoulders as he scooped ice cream would be dessert enough for some women. She wasn't one of them. Thank heavens she'd learned young how dangerous it was to allow oneself to be carried away by feelings. A pretty face could not influence her.

Not that Fletcher Kingsley was "pretty." She cocked her head as he squirted whipped cream on the sundaes. He was more handsome and kind of...sculpted. When he fished two maraschino cherries from a silver tray, she noticed that for a large man his fingers were fairly graceful and nimble and when he wisely served both boys at the same time, she forgave him his earlier manners. The giant, delighted grin on Orlando's face was a gift to her heart. Even Will, as serious as he could be, examined the mountain of ice cream, which looked to be way more than one scoop, with something akin to awe.

"How about you?"

Focused on her boys and her fervent desire to gain some financial stability so that she could give them this simple indulgence without needing a handout, Claire didn't realize at first that Fletcher was speaking to her.

"Well?" he said. "What'll it be?" When she gazed at him in confusion, he gestured to the double rows of ice cream tubs in the glass-topped freezer unit.

"Oh!" Claire shook her head. "No. Thank you very much, but...no."

"You don't like ice cream?"

"She loves it," Orlando said with his mouth full. "It's her favorite food after broccoli." He scooped up a malt ball and began to *zoom* it through the air on his spoon. Will followed suit with the maraschino cherry.

With the boys occupied, Fletcher ambled toward her end of the long marble bar. Though he clearly tried to walk normally, his gait was not smooth, and Claire found herself wondering when and how he had injured himself and whether it still hurt.

He stopped in front of her, stone-faced, but his voice carried a wry twist. "I can't compete with broccoli, but there are twenty flavors to choose from. Or there used to be." Almost lazily, his gaze homed in on her face. "See one of your favorites?"

Claire's mouth felt dry and uncomfortable; she had to force her tongue to form letter sounds. "Thank you, but..." She wasn't sure why it seemed important to decline, but knew she didn't want to take anything from him for herself. "No ice cream for me. I'm still...losing baby weight."

His eyes, too dark to read easily, scanned what he could see of her body, which wasn't much. Her coat and Rosalind covered her well.

One deep black brow hooked like a question mark. His lids lowered as if he'd grown sleepy, but she had the feeling he was as alert as a tiger at an antelope buffet.

"Your figure's fine. And you don't want to teach that little one—" he gestured toward Rosalind with the silver ice-cream scoop he'd picked up before walking her way "—to deny herself one of life's finest pleasures because she's worried about the size of her jeans."

Twin threads of pleasure and discomfort muddled Claire's brain.

Just a little ice cream—that's all it was from his perspective, but not from hers. She wasn't sure why, but an ice cream cone from Fletcher Kingsley would seem like an apple in the Garden of Eden.

"It's not even lunchtime." She cringed a little as the words escaped. Her mother had been right; she sounded like a schoolmarm.

"Do you like Moose Tracks?"

"Moose tracks. The animal moose?"

The corner of his mouth curled. "The flavor Moose Tracks."

"I don't know. I usually buy Neapolitan. That way everyone gets something they want."

He shook his head. "Well, that settles it."

Suddenly Fletcher seemed like a different man. His gaze turned speculative. The edge of danger remained, but missing was the sense that he was going to bolt at any moment. He seemed to have all the time in the world as he gazed at her. His silence made her nervous.

"What?" she asked. "What are you looking at?"

"He's trying to figure out your signature sundae."

Claire turned. Dean stood behind her, a smile on his handsome face. Crossing his arms over his chest, he tipped his head toward her and murmured in a loud "whisper" his brother could hear, "He used to do this when he worked the fountain in high school. Fletcher has an uncanny knack for knowing exactly which flavors someone will love. It's a gift."

While Fletcher removed the lids on a couple of the large jars lining the counter, Dean provided the color play. "Right now he's trying to sense exactly which dry topping is right for you. Peanut brittle? Mini white chocolate chips? Who is Claire, and what is her sundae?"

Dean sounded like a TV commentator. He made it all sound so mysterious and suspenseful that Claire giggled.

"Will he choose the butterscotch morsels?" Dean asked, letting anticipation hover in the air before he answered himself. "No. He's still wondering."

"What I'm wondering," Fletcher said without looking their

way, "is how we could have the same blood running through our veins."

With a brilliant deftness, he used the tip of the silver scoop to fling a nonpareil at Dean. The chocolate disk sailed through the air in a perfect arc, allowing Dean to move forward only slightly in order to catch it in his mouth.

"See what I mean?" he said to Claire after he had chewed. "The high school girls used to mob this place. By three-fifteen, every stool would be filled with girls waiting for Fletch to make them a personalized sundae. My brother could have been the Emeril Lagasse of the soda fountain, but he didn't think it was exciting enough."

"Imagine that," Fletcher muttered.

A string of bells jingled against the glass door to the pharmacy. "That's my cue to get back to work," Dean said, setting a stack of white bar towels on the marble counter and suggesting to Fletcher, "Call if you don't have plans tonight. We can grab dinner."

Fletcher emitted a decidedly noncommittal grunt and then got serious about Claire's ice cream.

She watched him, wondering what career he'd chosen instead of working behind the soda fountain, why he and his brother—who seemed like a man of true quality—weren't as close as they should be, and why she hadn't heard before today that Dean Kingsley had a brother. Her neighbor Irene seemed to know most everything about Honeyford and all its residents and regularly filled Claire in.

Working a soda fountain seemed like a good job. Claire had no siblings, but if she'd had one like Dean Kingsley, she'd have been happy as a clam to toil the day away in a family business. Being part of a respectable, close-knit clan that took care of each other and was thought of highly in their community—that seemed like heaven to her. Then again, she'd never wanted the moon. A modest piece of earth, enough food to eat and a happy family was all she'd asked for.

Dean obviously wanted his brother's company. Fletcher behaved as if he didn't return the feeling, but, she wondered, how much of that was an act? She thought about this morning and realized that his bark was much worse than his bite.

Engrossed in the construction of her sundae, Fletcher didn't glance at her again as he scooped up some kind of vanilla ice cream with a caramel-colored ribbon running through it. He drizzled a liquid topping over the perfect ball of ice cream, covered it in whipped cream from a can and then sprinkled on two different toppings. Slipping two fingers under the stem of the sundae glass, he set it on a plate, added a spoon and carried it to her.

He nodded toward Rosalind. "Can you sit with her strapped to you like that?"

Claire glanced at the boys. They were still enjoying themselves, absorbed in making their gummy worms wind around their spoons. She would have to clean up after them later, but for now Rosalind was still sleeping, and she was dead on her feet, so except for the conscience that made her want to pay her own way, there seemed to be no reason not to indulge herself with this small luxury.

Scooting onto the stool in front of her, she waited for him to set the plate down and walk away. He did the former, but remained where he was, crossing his arms over his chest, obviously waiting.

Claire didn't know whether she was nervous because she hadn't eaten with another adult in almost a year or because *he* was the adult watching her.

"Are you going to stand there while I eat?" she asked.

His head jerked back a bit, the way the boys' sometimes did when she caught them falling asleep in the car or in front of a video. "No." He uncrossed his arms and started to walk away.

"Because I don't mind if you're eating, too, but otherwise…it's just a little ooky."

He stopped, stared at her a moment and then didn't bother to mask the sardonic humor that made his wide, well-sculpted mouth curl. "Ooky, huh? Wouldn't want that." He unscrewed the lid on a jar of chocolate chips, scooped some into his palm and crossed back to her. He shook a few of the candies into his mouth then gestured to the creation in front of her. "Go on. Taste it."

Self-conscious, but knowing that fair was fair, she picked up her utensil and tried to pull off a ladylike serving. Fletcher made a sound of disgust.

"Not like that." Taking the spoon without her permission, he filled it with a little bit of every ingredient he'd put in the sundae then handed it back to her. "You need the full effect or my efforts have been wasted."

"Wouldn't want that," she echoed him, doing her best with the large spoonful. As the ice cream melted in her mouth, she began to taste…home.

Her eyes widened in surprise. One bite proved this was no mere sundae; it was a sweet symphony of flavors that, in combination, reminded her of all the homey warmth and comfort she craved. As the pillow of whipped cream dissolved, she began to recognize cinnamon…and caramel… vanilla…soft, sweet graham-cracker crumbs and…what?… apple. Yes, like a pie. The textures were equally delightful— airy, rich, creamy, chewy; there was even some crunch.

Over the past year, she'd eaten from a sense of duty. She'd been nourishing a baby and had to take care of herself to be of service to her kids. But, truly, eating had been just another chore.

Courtesy demanded that she give Fletcher the compliment

he was waiting for, but she wanted another bite. This time she didn't worry about manners and spooned up enough of the sundae to see if the second bite would be as good as the first, and it was.

She closed her eyes.

From the age of twelve, Claire's chief goal in life had been to stir and sustain inside herself a feeling of home and hearth, of comfort and care. A perpetual fantasy Thanksgiving. That feeling, absent throughout her childhood, had remained elusive for her even as an adult. Marrying Arlo had helped. Having children helped still more, but something always got in the way. Laundry piled up. The budget wouldn't balance. The house was always a tad more shabby than cozy. Arlo had never seemed to notice that something was missing, and she'd secretly felt guilty for wanting more when life had finally given her so much, but the perfect sense of home had continued to dodge her, and she had gone on wanting.

Now one of Fletcher Kingsley's signature sundaes had gotten it exactly right—the very feeling she'd longed for since she was old enough to dream. And Claire realized why that affected her so much.

*Fletcher has an uncanny knack for knowing exactly which flavors someone will love. It's a gift.... Who is Claire, and what is her sundae?*

She opened her eyes.

He was still watching her, but his smile was gone. He stood perfectly still.

"How do you know?" Her voice was a whisper, no stronger than the whipped cream. "How do you know what a total stranger is like?" She'd meant to say "what a total stranger *will* like," but this was more accurate.

Fletcher frowned and started to speak, and for a moment she thought he might deny having any such knowledge. Then his chest rose and fell on a sigh. He stared at her a moment longer. "You were easy."

He turned, wiped his hands on a bar towel and left without saying goodbye to the boys or cleaning the fountain area as his brother had asked. Claire knew without having to think about it that his actions were deliberate rather than oversight.

She was tempted to turn and watch him walk away, but restrained herself. Fletcher Kingsley craved solitude.

Which made her wonder. As shy as she sometimes felt, she craved community, togetherness. He was her polar opposite. Yet, for a moment, long enough to make a silly sundae that was melting even as she stared at it, he had understood.

Claire smiled ironically. She'd been validated by an ice cream sundae. Her life really did need work.


At Bumble's Bar and Grill, the coffee was almost bitterly strong, which was exactly what Fletcher needed after a long, frustrating day. He sat at the bar in the dark lounge, eschewing alcohol in favor of the caffeine and a turkey dinner.

After leaving the pharmacy, he'd done some shopping at the hardware store then paid a visit to Lanny Morgan at *The Buzz* to see if he could squeeze any information out about that ad.

Lanny swore he'd thrown out the original instructions, that they were typed and gave no clue as to who sent the ad in to the paper anyway. Lanford had filled out quite a bit in the ten years Fletcher had been way, lost that Ichabod Crane look, but he hadn't abandoned his obvious mistrust and dislike of Fletcher. Lanford's opinion had never bothered Fletcher before, but today it rankled.

"Here ya go. Turkey special." The bartender, a tall blonde with blue eyes and skin the color of a latte, set the plate before him.

"Thanks."

The turkey dinner was large and warm, and though it was only three o'clock in the afternoon, Fletcher had been starving when he'd walked in. Preparing decent meals was not his forte, and he'd missed lunch completely today. He picked up his fork then felt the bartender's gaze upon him. When he looked up, she was grinning.

"You really don't remember me, do you?"

His eyes fell to her nametag. "Sophie," it read. Neither the name nor the face rang a bell with Fletcher, but he figured she was about his age. Oh, man, he hoped he hadn't dated her, although if she'd lived in Honeyford during her high school years and she'd been available, the chances were good that he had.

Immediate discomfort killed the appetite he'd brought in.

"It's been a long time since I lived here, Sophie," he said in a quiet voice. Setting the fork on his plate, he straightened. He'd been a lousy boyfriend. Offhand, he could think of several girls whose feelings he had treated carelessly, dating them then moving on with no explanation that when emotions became involved, he became too uncomfortable to stay.

He'd come back to claim what was rightfully his, and he was honest enough to know there was as much rage as justice in his heart, but he realized, too, that he owed a few innocent people amends. He guessed he was about to start.

Resting his elbows on the bar, he met her eyes. "I don't remember you, Sophie, which says more about me a decade ago than it does about you. Do I have anything to apologize for?"

Her thickly lashed eyes popped wide open. Unusually white teeth sparkled as she giggled. "You went out with my sister, Emily. In eleventh grade. I was a freshman, but I used to follow you around school, trying to get you to notice me. Em's married with three little ones now, but I am completely available." She flipped the lid up on a divided tray and filled it with stuffed olives while she spoke to him. "I follow rodeo." Her cheeks dimpled as she slid him a knowing glance. "You're pretty much a local celebrity, cowboy. Although you were something of a celeb in high school, too."

He laughed outright at that. "For all the wrong reasons."

"Depends on your point of view." A slash of daylight illuminated the establishment's dark interior, and her gaze shifted to the entrance. "Rats. Business calls. 'Scuse me." She ducked beneath the bar's pass-through, popping up next to him, where she gave him enough time to notice that she'd matured well. "I get off at five today, by the way. Maybe you should eat slowly."

Her meaning was unmistakable. Fletcher was grateful that none of the other seats at the bar were currently occupied. The days when he'd relished attention, positive or negative, were over.

As the blonde moved off, he glanced at his meal. What he wanted was to ask for a to-go box, so he could eat at home.

Slicing a piece of turkey, he forced himself to taste the meal. He didn't intend to linger over it, and he definitely wasn't going anywhere with Sophie. As attractive as she was and as long as it had been since he'd had sex, no desire stirred inside him. Even if it had, he wasn't sure he'd do anything about it. Life was complicated enough.

This morning, his reaction to Claire Dobbs had thrown him for a loop.

The turkey began to lose its taste. He reached for the coffee instead.

That story about his knowing exactly what kind of sundae customers at the soda fountain liked was a bunch of crap, something he'd dreamed up in high school to make himself feel important and to score with girls. They'd liked the attention; no one had ever sent back a "signature" sundae, although he doubted he'd guessed right every time.

Today had been different. What had begun as a harmless conciliation had turned into a startling and disturbing discovery: he really had known what to make for Claire.

Old-Fashioned Apple Pie Ice Cream, a swirl of caramel, a sprinkle of graham-cracker crumbs, whipped cream and cinnamon chips. Home sweet home, but with enough spice to keep things interesting.

He clutched the coffee mug too tightly, realized it was cold when what he wanted was something scalding. He wondered how he could get more coffee without asking Sophie.

Prior to his injury this past summer, Fletcher had enjoyed an active but sane sex life. Always used a condom, had sex with one woman at a time and never, never got involved in the first place unless he was certain the woman understood that neither his companionship nor his performance in bed meant their relationship was going to turn permanent. There were enough women—usually a bit younger or a lot older than he—who were likewise happy to avoid marriage and family ties; he had always been able to scratch that particular itch.

The past year, though, sex had left him more restless than satisfied. He thought about Sophie, about her long legs and inviting smile and felt nothing, not a stir. It had been that way since his accident.

Until this morning.

Standing behind the counter of a soda fountain he loathed, serving up ice creams—which he loathed doing—he'd glanced at Claire Dobbs and suddenly his blood had started flowing again.

"You can drop the pies on that table there, and I'll get your money."

Unselfconscious, Sophie didn't mind that her voice rang through the lounge. Fletcher set his coffee cup down and filled his fork with mashed potatoes to deter conversation, but he needn't have bothered. From the corner of his eye, he saw her duck behind the bar, slip a piece of paper into the cash register and withdraw a few bills. Then she scooted beneath the pass-through again.

From somewhere behind him, he heard Sophie tell the new arrival, "We've got a party of twelve here on Sunday. Bum wants to know if you can make a couple of chocolate cakes and check in with us late Saturday to see if we need more pie."

Fletcher heard a feminine groan and then, "I'd love to. But my oven broke. I had to finish these off at a neighbor's, and I don't know if I can impose like that again so soon."

The forkful of lumpy spuds stopped halfway to Fletcher's mouth.

"Can't you get the oven fixed?" Sophie asked, though she sounded slightly bored.

Fletcher waited for the response, anticipating the Southern-accented voice with a fusion of interest and dread that made him feel like a kid who was promised a lollipop if he went calmly to the dentist.

"Not today," Claire Dobbs lamented. "And for sure not this weekend. I don't have the kind of cash to pay weekend rates."

"Okay. I'll tell Bum."

From Sophie's tone, Fletcher could tell the conversation was over in her mind. But Claire was a fighter.

"Maybe you could ask him if I can make the cakes here? I could come in early so I'm not in the way of your regular cooks. And I'll clean up after myself."

"I don't know," Sophie said, sounding doubtful. "Maybe. Bum's not here, but I'll leave him a note."

"Thanks," Claire murmured, clearly wanting to say more. Fletcher told himself to mind his own business, but his ears perked up again when she questioned, "Um, do you know if Bum is hiring right now? In the restaurant, I mean?"

"Don't think so, but you can fill out an app. Why don't you come back tomorrow?"

"I'd rather do it tonight, if that's all right. Get a jump on it."

"Bum keeps the applications in his office, honey. I don't know where they are."

Fletcher heard the strain in Claire's upbeat tone when she pressed, "I think I'll leave him a note asking if I can use the kitchen and then mention that I'm looking for work, too." It sounded as if she began rustling through her purse. "I have a pen and paper here. That way he'll be expecting me when I come in to fill out an application."

"Have you cocktailed before?" Sophie's tone expressed doubt, and Fletcher stiffened.

"I waited tables in a coffee shop," came the reluctant reply and then more quickly and more fiercely, "But I'm a fast learner. And a good worker."

Sophie laughed a little, and Fletcher wanted to gag her. "Okay. Well, write away. You can leave the note on the bar when you're through."

"Thank you."

Every muscle in Fletcher's shoulders and back tensed as he hunched over his plate. Claire Never-Say-Die Dobbs appeared to be determined to get a job today no matter where she had to apply, but he doubted Bum was hiring. After only two weeks in town, he recognized the signs of ongoing recession everywhere he went.

*Do not turn around,* he growled at himself, shoving the potatoes into his mouth. *Do not. This woman is not your responsibility.*

White cotton stretching across a calendar-worthy bosom entered his peripheral vision.

"You haven't made much of a dent in that meal, cowboy." Sophie leaned an elbow on the bar and swayed her hips, wiggling her fetching rump.

He heard Claire's pen scratch across paper and decided it would be safer to pay attention to Sophie.

Though they were several yards to the right of Claire, Fletcher made sure to keep his voice low. "Apparently I wasn't as hungry as I thought. I'll take this to go."

"I've got a better idea," Sophie plucked the fork from his hand. "My roommate is in Portland until Monday. Come to my place and keep me company while I make my famous lasagna. Then while it's in the oven, we can relax together, or you could show me some of your rodeo moves." Dipping the tines of his fork into the potatoes, she put it in her mouth, closed her lips around it and slowly dragged it out, clean as a whistle. Her super-sized blue eyes remained locked on him the entire time. "Could you teach me to rope something? I've always thought I'd be real good at that."

Fletcher had to laugh. "You're already good at it."

She grinned.

As the prodigal black sheep of Honeyford, Oregon, Fletcher knew his part well. This was the point at which his blood should begin to rush, as much from the thrill of the game as the need for sex. He wouldn't find a more willing partner; she wasn't even making him work for it.

Sex with Sophie would help him reestablish who he was in Honeyford—a man who lived on the fringe rather than inside the close-knit conservative community.

He stood and reached for his wallet.

Sophie straightened, a gorgeous, wild confidence and steady sexual hunger in her eyes. Here was a woman who obviously separated the physical from the emotional. They would be a good match.

Fletcher felt older than his age, suddenly, and tired, but

he relied on habit to pull up a smile of pure masculine appreciation. "How about a raincheck? I'm sure your lasagna is first-class, but there's something I have to do tonight."

Claire kept her head bent toward the note she was supposed to be writing, but her discreetly raised gaze devoured the scene at the bar. She tried not to eavesdrop, but simply couldn't resist.

Though the bar and lounge were dark, she had recognized Fletcher Kingsley the moment Sophie began to flirt with him. At first, the hunch of his shoulders and the fact that he was alone in a bar with a full plate of food in front of him had made him look sad, so she'd continued to stare. And to think.

His house had been in disrepair on the outside and lacked a sense of hominess inside. After this morning at the pharmacy, she had begun to suspect he lived by himself in the uninviting home, and her heart had strangely ached for the tough-talking man who made up lies about free ice cream so he could apologize without embarrassing himself.

In her mind, no one wanted to be completely solitary, no matter what they said. Life baked a hard crust over the hearts of some people, but that didn't mean they *liked* to be by themselves. Or cranky.

If he'd given her a job, she could have turned that big ranch into someplace welcoming. Someplace he would be proud to invite his brother over for Sunday dinner or for snacks and a laughter-filled game of cards. She could have filled the kitchen with food he'd be happy to come home to after a hard day's work.

Deliberately returning her gaze to the note she was penning to Bum, the owner of Bumble's Bar and Grill, Claire reminded herself to keep her eye on the ball.

Less than three hundred dollars remained in her bank

account. She had property taxes to pay, not to mention food and clothing to buy and plenty of other things that wishes would not fund. She couldn't waste time thinking about someone who wasn't planning to pay her salary, no matter how good he was at guessing which ice cream she wanted to eat, how generous he'd been with her boys or how much he reminded her of an old-fashioned movie star once he shaved and combed his hair.

Fletcher must have said something real pleasing at that moment, because Sophie laughed like she was happier than a bear at a picnic, and Claire's stubborn eyes refused to obey orders. Instead of focusing on the ball the way they were supposed to, they rose to watch Sophie toss her head, sending streams of hair that looked like melted butter over one shoulder. The knowledgeable blonde topped that move off with a smile that shone like a lighthouse beam, and an unwelcome pang of jealousy stabbed Claire. She didn't know the first thing about sending a man into a state of carnal desire just by shaking her head.

In her entire life, she had made love with one man. She didn't regret that fact, but she and Arlo had been like an old married couple from the beginning—comfortable and sweet. She had no idea how to seduce a man in broad daylight, in a public place the way Sophie was doing.

Beneath his dark green shirt, Fletcher's broad shoulders moved restlessly. Probably he was getting ready to jump over the bar.

An uncomfortable, prickly heat crawled through Claire's veins as she watched the blonde continue to flirt with Fletcher. Rightly identifying the feeling as envy, she recoiled from it.

Determinedly finishing her note, she began to hum to herself so she wouldn't even think about the scene in front of her.

The conversation got quieter.

A glass thunked as it was set on the bar.

The legs of a wooden stool scraped across the floor.

Claire folded her sheet of paper, wrote Bum's name on top, and hoped the couple would go away before she had to place the note on the bar. Reaching for the purse she'd deposited by the side of her chair, she hummed a little louder.

"I can name that tune in five notes."

The wry male voice floated to her from somewhere above her head.

Claire looked up to see Fletcher hooking his suede coat over his shoulder like a cowboy in a cigarette ad, the same enigmatic expression as before in his dark eyes.

Her heart pounded hard as she straightened in her seat. "I beg your pardon?"

"The Star-Spangled Banner," he guessed. "That's what you're humming, isn't it?"

Claire had to think a minute. "Yes."

"A favorite of yours or are you feeling patriotic?"

He had one of the deepest voices Claire had ever heard. She had to remember how much she preferred soft-spoken gentleman whose tones were sensitive and sweet to men who sounded as if they could crush steel girders without breaking a sweat.

Irritated with herself for feeling nervous around him, she rose and swung her purse onto her shoulder. "You never know when you'll be asked to sing at a ball game."

Appreciation flashed in his otherwise shuttered expression. "You're very practical."

"Yep." She gave him a neighborly nod. "It's nice to see you again. I've got to get back home."

"Mind if I tag along?"

Claire blinked, stupid with surprise. "What?"

He stood like a mountain, composed and steady. "I heard

you mention that your oven is out. I thought I'd take a look at it."

It took a moment to decide she'd heard him correctly and another moment to decide he wasn't kidding.

"You want to look at my oven." As always when her emotions were high, her accent became more pronounced, and "my oven" emerged, "m'oven."

His mountain lips curled ever so slightly. "If you don't mind. I'm fairly good with electrical appliances."

"And you want to do this *now?*" She craned her neck to look for Sophie then remembered he wasn't supposed to know she'd been eavesdropping.

Fletcher used one finger to scratch his cheek. "If I recall correctly, I liked to eat when I was a little boy. I imagine you're going to need that oven again soon."

That was true. And, if he fixed the oven tonight, she could bake the cakes for Bum this weekend. It was a good deal from her perspective. But from his…?

"Are you sure?"

"I am." He nodded to the paper in her hand. "Are you finished with your note?"

He didn't seem to mind at all letting her know that he'd listened to her conversation. She turned the yellow paper over in her hands. "I have to leave this on the bar. I wonder where Sophie went?"

"She's getting something for me."

Claire barely had time to wonder what before the blonde pushed through the kitchen door holding a plastic bag, knotted at the top. Inside, there appeared to be a stack of to-go boxes.

"Here ya go, handsome," she said as she walked toward them. Fletcher reached for the bag. Sophie held on as their fingers touched. "I wrote my phone number on the top box." A sexy dimple appeared in one cheek. "You can't miss it."

The blonde released the bag slowly, and Claire watched in sheer awe as long, French-manicured nails traced a wavy line along the back of Fletcher's hand up to his wrist. Sophie would have gone further, but the cuff was buttoned. When she drew her hand away, she pushed it through her hair, the gesture drawing attention to the golden locks while simultaneously stretching her white cotton tee more tightly across her bosom.

As if the scene were evolving on TV, Claire quickly looked to Fletcher to see what he was going to do.

The brown eyes remained dark and still as a pond at night, hiding whatever lurked below the surface.

"Thanks." He carried the plastic bag with a couple of fingers hooked in the loops.

That was it. That was all he was going to say. But he smiled, and that seemed to be enough for Sophie. She gave him a confident wink.

"Put that phone number in your cell so you don't lose it." She inched closer. "And my guess is you'll be using it *a lot*."

Mesmerized by the unabashed display, Claire stood alongside Fletcher, watching Sophie walk away, her perfect, jeans-clad bottom swaying provocatively.

She looked up at the object of all that feminine affection. "Fixing my oven seems like a mighty strange choice for a man who just got a much better offer."

"Don't analyze it."

With a heart that felt much lighter than it had a few minutes ago, Claire shrugged. "Okay."

## Chapter Five

Claire asked Fletcher to wait while she set her note next to the cash register. When she returned, he preceded her to the door and held it open. They stepped into perfect fall sunshine and an apple-crisp chill.

Claire loved Honeyford's Main Street. Buildings that looked as if they hadn't been upgraded in a hundred years stood shoulder to shoulder with shop fronts clearly redesigned to honor the traditional while achieving a more updated and, in a few cases, upscale appearance. The barbershop, aptly named Honey Combs, was one of the structures that retained its original charms, including a red-and-white striped barber pole. As they passed by the business, Claire wondered what Fletcher would look like with his dark hair trimmed then decided the thick hanks falling below his collar were part of his bigger-than-life appeal.

And he was appealing to her, the way a celebrity appealed to an average Joe. She and Fletcher Kingsley had nothing in common. She was straightforward and simple; he was an amalgam of confusing and sometimes opposing traits that gave him an aura of mystery. Coupled with the intense sexuality that had smoldered across the bar, he was as out of her league as if they lived on different planets. Yet here they were, walking to her house together.

Sophie made her look like a kindergartener in the arena of feminine wiles, but she didn't need feminine wiles with Fletcher. As they headed down Main Street, she felt surprisingly upbeat and relaxed.

"So, do you have a girlfriend already?" she asked cheerfully. "Because that's the only way I see a man like you resisting Sophie. That girl has more tricks up her sleeve than a Vegas magician."

Fletcher erupted in laughter that was rich and real. Claire was pleased. It made his entire face soften.

"What do you know about Vegas magicians?" he asked.

"I lived in Las Vegas for one year." His brows rose, which also pleased her. She could have said more: that her mother had been a croupier in the casino at Circus Circus. That at age ten Claire had been thrilled her mother seemed finally to have a real job, and that she'd been so excited about the possibility they might stay put awhile she hadn't even minded... too much...that she'd had to stay alone at night in their rented apartment while Didi had worked.

"Have you ever been there?" she asked Fletcher, preferring not to remember that Las Vegas had turned out to be merely one more stop on a wearily long journey. Typically, Didi had pulled up stakes before a year was out.

"A time or two."

"Did you gamble when you were there?"

"Some."

"Were you there on business or pleasure?"

He glanced down at her, exasperation tingeing the corners

of his mouth. Clearly, he hoped to conduct their relationship with as few words as possible, but she wasn't going to let him get away with that. So when all he answered was, "Business," she asked, "Ranch business?"

He glanced down at her. "No."

They walked several more steps in silence, which gave her a chance to study the clean granite-hard angles of his face, and then in a tone she believed was deliberately surly he said, "Come on. You know you're not going to leave it at that."

She kept her smile inside and questioned sedately, "What kind of work were you doing in Vegas?"

She thought she caught the whisper of a smile before he responded, "Rodeo."

"Rodeo!" Surprise made her skip ahead, facing him, fists planted on her hips. "Were you behind the scenes or right out front?"

She walked backwards, and Fletcher slowed his pace so she wouldn't trip. Claire seemed impressed by the admission that he'd been on the rodeo circuit, but if she were truly a fan, she'd know exactly what he had done.

After a half-dozen national rodeo championships and almost twice as many records for bull riding, calf roping and saddle bronc riding, the advertising world had come courting. For over two years, his name and image had graced billboards, magazine ads, even the city bus as the face (and butt) of Tough Enuff jeans. He'd also done his part to sell Blue Velvet aftershave, Willamette Falls beer and Wild Roses lipstick, when they'd hired him to let four exuberant models kiss his cheeks repeatedly, leaving lip prints in a variety of hard-to-wipe-off hues. Living in—and more often dodging—the public eye had rapidly lost its appeal, but the money had been great and had suited Fletcher's goal to purchase and restore Pine Road Ranch.

His accident had killed his rodeo career, but Hollywood

loved drama, and lately his agent had been presenting him with offers to appear on everything from soap operas to a new cable western. It was refreshing to meet a woman under thirty who had no idea who he was, how much he was worth or how many parties he and George Clooney had both attended.

He studied her—open mouth, sparkling eyes and all—and wondered if she was going to turn groupie on him now. "I was right up front."

"Busting broncs and roping calves and everything?"

As jaded as he often felt, Fletcher smiled. Coming from a woman as ingenuous as Claire Dobbs, perhaps a little adulation wouldn't bother him. "Yeah, busting broncs and everything."

"I watched part of a rodeo on TV once. It seemed so cruel." Shaking her head, she fell into step beside him again. "I mean, the animals don't have a choice about being there, getting roped and kicked with those sharp pizza-cutter things—"

"Pizza cutter—you mean spurs?"

"Yes, spurs. They look nasty. And the humans have all the advantage."

Fletcher stopped dead. "Humans have all the advantage?" So much for adulation.

As much as he liked to avoid being sucked into unnecessary interactions, he couldn't let her comment go. "The spurs are dull. The animal doesn't feel a thing. And until you've been on top of a two-ton bull with anger issues, don't tell me who has the advantage."

Claire cocked her head. "Is that how you hurt your leg? On a bull with anger issues?"

This conversation was requiring a lot more talk than he'd intended when he'd first decided to look at her stove. "Yes."

She didn't come any higher than his shoulder as they

walked down Main Street in the cloyingly quaint town he'd once been so happy to leave for good.

"So you're going to be a rancher now?" she asked.

He was going to turn Pine Road Ranch into the envy of everyone in town. It wasn't exactly the same thing, but he nodded in the affirmative.

"That seems like a good life," she said. "You never answered my first question, you know."

"What first question? You ask so many, I can't keep track."

His deliberate gruffness bothered her not a bit if her wide smile was any indication. "The girlfriend question. Do you have one?"

"You're nosy. When I met you this morning, you didn't seem nosy."

"Sorry," she apologized cheerfully, looking way up at him. "I just don't know how a man could resist all that flirting back at the bar, that's all. Unless he's married or otherwise taken, of course, and you don't seem taken."

She kept watching him and finally Fletcher glanced down, raising a brow at her. "Sophie is working for the next hour and a half."

"Oh." She let that sink in a moment. "Where do you think you'll take her?"

"She invited me to her place, and how is that any of your business?"

Pressing her lips together, she thought before responding. "Shoot, I can't think of a single reason. But I was married before I could vote, and I'm as backwards as a car in reverse when it comes to dating. I've got to pick up some knowledge before my children grow up and get curious. They're bound to ask me all sorts of questions that I can't answer."

"You're planning on dating so you can answer your kids' questions?"

"Of course not." She shook her head vehemently. "I'm not planning on dating, ever. That's why I'm so nosy. It's you or reality TV, and I can't afford cable."

She'd done it again—pulled an honest-to-God laugh out of him, the kind that came to Fletcher so rarely it was like a new acquaintance rather than an old friend.

They'd reached the end of the block, and he was about to ask whether her house was in town or they needed to drive there in his truck when a middle-aged man sweeping the sidewalk in front of Bee-lieve Inspirational Bookstore looked up and did a swift double take. Behind thin-rimmed glasses, the gentleman, wearing neatly pressed beige trousers and a green-and-white-striped button-down shirt, blinked hard at Fletcher.

"Kingsley," he grunted, leaving no doubt that a hero's welcome was not forthcoming. Fletcher saw the man's pale, freckled fingers tighten around the handle of his broom. "I heard you were back." He waited, as if he expected the brusque comment to encourage conversation.

Fletcher nodded and replied only, "Mr. Garlock."

The other man's face twisted with blatant dislike. He pressed his lower lip into his top lip, forming an unhappy upside-down *U*. His chin quivered as if he were trying to hold back words until finally the dam burst. "Davy is trying to get back on his feet." Red-faced, he sputtered, "He doesn't need you messing with his head. You...you stay away from my boy."

Every muscle in Fletcher's body tensed, and the small amount of dinner he'd had turned sour in his stomach. "I haven't seen Davy in ten years, Mr. Garlock."

"It doesn't matter. You were always poison to him. You stay away, you hear me?"

Fletcher heard Claire gasp beside him. He felt seventeen again, walking with a girl and knowing there wasn't a father in town that wanted good-for-nothing Fletcher Kingsley to spend time with his daughter.

In high school, Davy Garlock and Fletcher had dubbed themselves the Dastardly Duo, causing as much trouble as they dared without breaking the law. Then, during their senior year, Davy had gotten into drugs. Miraculously, Fletcher had realized that drugs would be more trouble than he could handle, plus he had an aversion to anything pharmaceutical. When he left town after graduation, he and Davy lost touch. Despite the fact that they had always fed off each other's confusion and discontent, it had pained Fletcher then and it pained him now to think that his friend waged a battle with drugs.

But Don Garlock wouldn't want to hear that.

Fletcher was about to signal to Claire that they needed to move on when she stretched out her right hand.

"Hello, Mr. Garlock. I'm Claire Dobbs." Although her tone was sweet and friendly, a glance at her face showed the determined expression Fletcher recognized from this morning. "I don't believe we've met yet. I'm new to town. Been here a little over two months, and I'm as happy as can be to call Honeyford my home." Her smile stretched wider, giving Fletcher a glimpse of the charm and guile of which she was capable. "I've been looking forward to browsing through your shop. I'd come in and pick up something to read right now if it weren't for the fact that Mr. Kingsley is coming over to fix my broken oven, which is downright generous of him since I can't afford to hire a repairman. Maybe I can stop by your store with my kids tomorrow. Do you have a children's section?"

Donald Garlock's lips unlocked only long enough for him to blubber, "Uh…yes." Awkwardly, he accepted Claire's outstretched hand. Fletcher felt a small tug on his arm, as if she expected him to stick his hand out as well. He knew better.

Garlock would rather sever Fletcher's fingers than shake his hand in goodwill.

Remaining rooted to the sidewalk while Claire exercised her public relations skills, Fletcher realized he'd been viewing her as a private, somewhat diffident woman whose vulnerability was bound to be a disadvantage for her.

Now something stirred inside him, some long dormant awareness that left him touched by this innocent young woman. In so many ways she seemed not to care about what others thought of her. Yet she stuck her neck way out for her kids and now for him, too, a virtual stranger.

Claire didn't know he probably deserved the bad opinion Donald Garlock had of him. Moreover, Fletcher understood in a flash that she wouldn't care. Despite the circumstances of their first meeting, she had decided he was worth defending.

Because he didn't want to feel touched by her concern, he tried to tell himself she had an angle; everyone had an angle. But the conscience he thought he'd killed off long ago pricked him. Doubting Claire Dobbs's sincerity was like believing in killer butterflies.

The moment she finished greeting Garlock, he started to walk. Still holding his arm, she was tugged along in his wake.

Refusing to entertain any questions or conversation about what had just transpired, Fletcher braced himself to cut her off at the knees if she said a word.

On the corner of Third and Main, he opened his mouth to ask which direction her house was in. She beat him to the punch. "I'm a few blocks up on Fourth." Pointing south, she left it at that, no Southern-accented questions or comments.

He limped across Main as quickly as he could, forcing her to trot a little to stay abreast of him. When they reached the far curb and stepped up, his hip protested the brisk pace, and he stumbled. Claire's arm curled tightly around his, bracing him.

Fletcher wanted to believe he saved himself from falling, but she was stronger than she looked. Her grip helped him rebalance.

Offering a gruff "Thank you," he pulled away.

"Well, that wasn't using my head at all, was it?" Pressing her knuckles to her hips, she looked annoyed with herself. "Of course you shouldn't walk that far. Where's your cane, anyway? Oh, never mind. You probably didn't want it when you were courting Sophie." She looked around. "Are you parked nearby?"

Fletcher didn't know what to laugh at first: the notion of his "courting" someone, or the idea that he would care if a woman he was interested in saw him with a cane.

His ego didn't work that way. It wouldn't bother him a bit if every attractive, available female between Oregon and the Atlantic states knew he needed a cane to climb a curb. What turned his blood cold was the possibility that his brother and people like Garlock would see him struggle.

"It's not a problem. I'll walk," he said.

"No, it's uphill," Claire protested. "We can go back and get your car. You must have driven into town. Or, you can meet me there, if you want. I'll walk on ahead."

"I'm walking."

"That's plain silly. You shouldn't do anything to hurt yourself."

From the corner of his eye, he saw movement in the window of the Hair Hive. A quick glance told him that two faces were pressed to the glass, watching him with Claire.

"Keep walking," he directed, pulling her along. Another half block, and they'd be on a residential street where, hopefully, the majority of busybodies would be inside or at work.

Claire stopped cold, facing him, "Mr. Kingsley, how are you going to get better if you don't take care of yourself?"

"Ms. Dobbs, who said I was going to get better?" Instantly, her expression rearranged itself into a sympathetic look that made him want to climb out of his skin. "You're fussy. I hate fussing." He stepped around her to continue up the street. "Did you mother your husband like this?"

It was a clumsy, rude remark he regretted immediately, and he half hoped Claire would tell him to go to hell. Instead her mobile features settled into a pensive frown as she resumed walking. "I never thought about it. Probably I did. Arlo never said anything, but then, he wouldn't have."

*Fine. Good. Sorry I mentioned it.* Except that now she looked worried.

"Why?" he barked. "If it bothered him, why wouldn't he have mentioned it?"

"Well, Arlo liked to talk, so it's not that we didn't communicate. It's just that he wasn't the type to complain. He wouldn't have said anything regardless. He needed mothering, and that's what I'm best at, so I suppose we were a good fit all around."

He glanced over, knowing he shouldn't. A sad, wistful smile made her mouth prettier than lipstick could have.

"I know that's not very exciting." She shrugged, looking not at all embarrassed or apologetic. "Like I said, I don't get out much."

Then she grinned sweetly up at him, and Fletcher's breath caught like a fishhook in the middle of his chest. She looked… fresh…pure. She looked like no one he had ever known.

He shook his head to clear it. What the devil was the matter with him today? Years ago he'd snuffed hope out of his soul with the same careless intent he'd use to crush a cigarette butt with the heel of his boot. Vengeance, not friendship was his purpose in returning to this godforsaken town. Damned if he'd let a woman who didn't know better than to trust a complete stranger louse things up for him.

*I'll look at her oven, and then I'm done.*

He made absolutely certain not to glance her way again as he trudged the blocks to her house, prepared to get this good-neighbor business over with once and for all.

Irene Gould was standing in the short entry hall of Claire's home, her bony hands clutching a heavily bundled Rosalind. Claire knew immediately that something was wrong.

"Thank heavens you're back! I was about to take the baby to Doctor Rollins. I made a call, and they can see her if we get there right away—"

"What's happening, Irene? Please, slow down. What's the matter?"

Claire rushed to take the baby, and the moment she did she knew what had agitated the normally unflappable older woman. Rosalind was burning up. Instead of crying from the discomfort of fever, she seemed listless, and her breathing was heavy with congestion.

The boys ran in from their bedroom, hats on and coats zipped. Ready to go.

"We got toys to keep us occupied!" Orlando spoke with wide eyes and his customary intense energy. "An' I branged George in case Rozzy wants to hold him, 'cause she is gonna cry when that doctor sticks a needle in her."

"She's not getting a shot," his brother corrected.

"Doctor's always give shots. Even when they say they're not gonna."

Will threw his arm around Orlando, which Claire recognized as his attempt to stop his brother's chatter. The older boy's hazel eyes looked decades older than they should have. "Rozzy's not going to die." Rather than asking a question,

Will spoke with the intensity of someone telling the universe how things were going to be.

"Of course she's not," Claire responded emphatically, but her heart was running a mile a minute. Her baby didn't even seem to care that Mama was holding her. "Irene, can you stay with the boys awhile longer?"

Amid a chorus of protests, the robust elderly woman agreed.

"Orlie, Will," Claire said, "I need you to stay here. You be sure Rozzy's crib is made for when we get back, and I would love it if you'd rake some of those front-yard leaves. That'd be a big, big help."

Both boys started to protest. Claire had tried to keep her request kind and encouraging, but from his place near the front door Fletcher said far more sternly, "They'll get on the job right away. Won't you, boys?"

Two hesitant, obviously reluctant nods followed his question. Claire headed for the door. As she started to pass through, Fletcher said, "I'll drive you."

The impulse to accept, to not have to do this alone was so strong Claire almost sobbed, "Yes." But one blinding moment of clarity made her state instead, "It'll be better if I do this on my own. I might be a while," she added under her breath, so the boys wouldn't hear. "If you're still willing to look at my oven, I'd appreciate it."

Fletcher looked as if he wanted to protest, but Irene said, "If you can get Claire's oven to work, I'll make dinner so there'll be something ready for when those boys get hungry."

As she brushed past Fletcher, Claire smelled his wonderful spicy cleanness and sensed his reluctance to let her leave on her own. Their gazes connected a bit too tightly, held on a moment too long, and for the barest instant she felt as if the two of them were in this together.

There would be moments like this from now on, moments she had to feel strong enough to navigate all by herself. If she took a crutch now, she'd look for another to lean on tomorrow and the day after that and the day after that.

"Thank you," she whispered.

Fletcher opened his mouth to speak, but Claire turned away, calling loudly over her shoulder, "I'll be back soon."

The spell was broken.

# Chapter Six

In the end, she was gone a total of two hours, during which she'd discovered her daughter had pre-pneumonia and that her bank account, after the office visit and prescription she had to pick up, was half gone. Their medical insurance from Arlo had ended the month before, and Claire's kids hadn't been approved yet for Oregon's state plan. Rosalind had perked up and was even breathing a bit easier, but Claire felt like crying. Or yelling. Or both.

She was about as tired as she'd ever been when she walked in her front door at almost six o'clock. The sky was dark and star dusted, with a sharp autumn chill that would have made her think of hot cider, crackling logs and a game of Go Fish if she hadn't been obsessing about work, money and…work. What good was this big old house if her children were going to starve beneath its roof? Or if she had to piece together so many small jobs to stay afloat that she was never home with them?

She would be hard-pressed to recall a day from her own childhood when she hadn't had to wonder where her mother was. Didi's jobs had kept her out at all hours, and then she'd stayed out longer still to "unwind." How many times had Claire made two peanut-butter sandwiches for dinner, one for herself and one for her mom, and then sat in their apartment, waiting? Eventually, she would eat what she could, battling against the nauseating fear of being alone.

Her grip on Rosalind unconsciously tightened until the baby squirmed. Arlo had promised Claire "always." Always to be together, always to hold hands so they could stand stronger against a battering wind.

In the past year, she had thumbed her nose at her fears, bullied them back, but tonight they felt like a geyser about to blow. She hardly ever allowed herself to think it, but what if she could not take care of her family? What if—

Closing her eyes briefly, feeling as if she might throw up, Claire shoved her key in the deadbolt.

"Hi, everyone. We're back!" she called as she entered the house. Tension roughened her voice, but she pushed a grateful smile to her lips, knowing she owed that, at least, to Irene Gould. The poor woman had been at the house for hours. That was another of Claire's worries: how to compensate the kind neighbor with something more than pies to share with Irene's bunko group.

Cacophonous whoops and hollers greeted Claire like a rush of warm air. The sounds emanated from the kitchen, from which the aroma of a hot meal also wafted. A smidgen of the tension eased. She'd been given a bright spot in this otherwise depressing day; her oven was fixed, and she could make the cakes for Bum.

"That smells so good, Irene!" Claire called above the noise as she dropped her purse, kicked off her outdoor shoes and began to unwrap the heavy clothing around Rosalind. "I just can't thank you enough!"

"Why don't you carry a cell phone?"

Rife with opinion, the question was spoken more like a statement, and it was definitely spoken by someone other than Irene.

Claire looked around. "Mr. Kingsley?" The dour-faced, jeans-clad cowboy stood in the archway between her dining and living rooms.

"Fletcher," he corrected. His hands sat on his slim hips as he glared at her. "Everyone carries a cell phone these days. Irene said you don't have one."

Setting Rosalind on the sofa with a faded blue rabbit to hold, Claire shrugged out of her coat. The room was as warm as a bath. Instantly, her tension mounted again.

Ignoring the cell-phone question—the answer to which should have been obvious—she complained, "It's hot in here. Is the heat up?"

"Damn right it's up. The house felt like a refrigerator. It's amazing you all don't have pneumonia. How's the baby?"

Guilt and then anger flared inside Claire. She heard the judgment in Fletcher's tone, and for a moment she wanted to blast him for it, but she managed to lock her lips against the pressure building inside her. He had done her a favor, and God knew she didn't have the energy for a fight. "Rosalind is going to be fine," she said tightly. "The doctor gave her an antibiotic and something to reduce the fever while we were still in the office. She's better already."

Hanging her coat and Rosalind's on the old mahogany coat tree, she spoke as she crossed back to her daughter. "Well, it smells like you fixed the oven. Thank you very much. I'm terribly sorry it took you so long." She scooped Rosalind up, wishing she could put all the kids to bed in the next five minutes and begin planning the cakes for Bum. Maybe that would relieve the stress damming up inside her. "Is Irene in the kitchen? I know she's playing cards tonight. I don't want her to be late."

There was a second archway, closer to her, which also led through the formal dining room and into the kitchen. She headed for that entrance, steering a wide path around Fletcher.

"She left half an hour ago," he informed, still with that disapproving air. "Apparently the game is at her house and couldn't be switched."

"You're here alone with the boys?" She stepped into the dining room, and he did the same.

"Ironic, isn't it?" They stared at each other across the length of the floral-papered room. "I couldn't fix the oven. The damn thing's a dinosaur. I think it needs a new starter, but they might have used twigs and matches when it was built."

"It worked just fine this morning." In her disappointment and her anxiety, Claire wanted to hit someone for the first time in her life. "It'll work again."

He hadn't fixed the oven! That meant no cakes for Bum unless Bum allowed her to use his kitchen. It also meant she had no way to bake the muffins and cookies she'd been peddling around town from the back of the boys' old Radio Flyer wagon.

Hysteria bubbled inside her. When Claire was thirteen, the Department of Human Services had finally caught up with her and Didi, mostly, Claire had always suspected, because she hadn't attended school regularly. Too many moves and too many anxious nights with no sleep had left her so far behind her peers that school had become a torture. By that time, Claire had taught herself to cook and bake in part as an effort to bring Didi home at night, and she had started to

take her plastic-wrapped offerings to any business she thought
might pay for a coffee-break snack.

Her small business had been somewhat profitable, but
the DHS didn't give extra credit to mothers whose teenage
daughters figured out how to fend for themselves. When the
social workers discovered that Didi could no longer pay the
utilities and that Claire was left unsupervised for days at a
time, Claire was put into state care. Foster homes were few
and far between for teenagers, so she was moved around
a lot. Quickly she learned that the terror of being alone in
an apartment belonging to her and her mother was nothing
compared to being unsure of exactly where she was when
she woke up in the morning. Didi visited her every now and
again, and Claire learned not to cry or beg to come home,
because if the visits were too difficult Didi wouldn't show up
again for a long time. The pattern of moves and sporadic Didi
visits continued on and off for two years until Didi regained
custody, moved them to Kentucky and told Claire not to cut
class unless she wanted to wind up singing Christmas carols
with the state again.

From that time on, she was as careful as she could possibly
be about making her home life appear normal to bystanders.
She never forgot the feeling of being taken from the only
parent she knew, even if the parent was Didi. Then she met
Arlo, spent all her free time with him, and, eventually, got
Didi's permission to marry at seventeen.

She'd made her own family, but now her dreams for her
children, the silent vows she had made the day each of them
was born, felt as if they were floating on choppy water, moving farther and farther from her reach. Worse still—far, far
worse—was the fear she had tried not to allow herself: What
if she could not take care of her children? What if the acorn
hadn't fallen far enough from the tree, and someone called
DHS about her?

Across the dining room, empty and unnecessarily lit with the electricity she couldn't afford, Claire glared at the rancher who dared to come into her home under the pretense of helping and then start criticizing her.

"A *skilled* repairman will have no trouble fixing that stove so that it'll run for another fifty years," she hissed, moving closer so she didn't have to shout above the boys' loud play. "And exactly what do you mean, 'no wonder she got sick'? I keep this house as warm as we need it." She stormed furiously toward the kitchen then turned and stormed furiously back, blood pumping with the near manic need to protect her small family. "Just for the record, I saw the bottle you were carrying around this morning. I'm positive it wasn't for show, so don't think anyone is going to listen to you if you say I'm an unfit mother. I am not unfit! And people got along just fine for centuries without cell phones!" Orlando shouted like a banshee in the kitchen. "What is going on in there, anyway?" Shooting daggers at the man in her dining room, who now looked far more like a danger than a potential friend, Claire carried Rosalind to the swinging kitchen door and pushed through.

She expected chaos, children who had taken full advantage of the lack of supervision. Although in Will's case that might be a good thing, the terrible lack of certainty in their lives propelled Claire to seek order anywhere she could get it, and she was ready to go into drill-sergeant mode. The sight that greeted her halted the orders she was about to bark.

The armless chairs around Aunt Faylene's old kitchen table had been pulled away and were now grouped two by two, facing each other so that the tufted cushions touched. It took only a couple of moments for Claire to realize the chairs were now "horses," on which her boys were riding. Yarn from her knitting basket wound around the chairs' ladder backs, providing the reins. A sponge mop was positioned to make the tail on William's horse; a broom substituted for the real thing on Orlando's. Over the boy's happy shouts, the timer on the microwave dinged.

Without a word, Fletcher edged past her to pull a plate from the countertop oven. Setting it aside, he put another full plate in and pressed the buttons. The microwave whirred to life again.

The boys looked around, saw her in the doorway and began talking, both at once.

"Look, Mom! I'm ridin' the range!" Orlando shouted, swirling an imaginary rope above his head. "I'm going to lasso me a bull. Yee-ha!"

Will climbed off his chairs and rushed over, prepared to abandon play in favor of being the big brother. "How is she, Mom?" He looked at Rosalind with concerned eyes that only a second ago had seemed uncharacteristically trouble free.

"She's going to be fine, son." Claire forced a smile as Will patted Rosalind's plump leg.

"We're having dinner now, Mom. I said we needed to wait, 'cause you'd be hungry, too, but he said—" Will shot a glance at Fletcher's back, and Claire could see that despite the fun and games he didn't fully trust the stern cowboy.

"Mr. Kingsley said," she corrected softly.

"Mr. Kingsley said dinner's getting dry as horse hair, and we got to eat it before we have to bury it." Will leaned in close and whispered, "I told him where the garbage pail is and that we don't bury food around here, but I don't think he listens good."

Claire nodded, torn between taking her little boy in her arms and hugging until he begged for freedom, and giving him the man-of-the-house response she knew he wanted. She settled on the latter option.

"I'm going to put Rozzy in her high chair. I think she's got an appetite now that she's feeling better. It'd be a big help if you cut up a banana for her while I help Mr. Fletcher with supper."

"Can I use a sharp knife?" Will asked hopefully.

"I think a butter knife will do for a banana."

While Will set about his task and Orlando rode the range, Claire settled Rosalind then approached the counter where Fletcher Kingsley was removing a second dish from the microwave.

Three plates, heaped with turkey, stuffing, potatoes and green peas sat side by side on the counter. A set of empty to-go containers with gravy dripping from their corners littered the yellow tile counter.

"You brought these from Bumble's," Claire stated, for the first time realizing that he and not Irene was providing her family's dinner. "You were carrying them when we walked home."

"They're still good. I had them in the refrigerator."

"Why?" she insisted. "Why did you buy us dinner? Were you afraid I couldn't feed my children?"

Her voice held that note of hysteria she'd successfully held back all year, but which now seemed determined to leak out. Fletcher's wide chest and broad shoulders stiffened as he picked up two of the plates.

"I'm going to put these on the table over there. I'll leave you to convince Orlando he's got to take apart those chairs and eat dinner. Then you and I are going to step back into the living room, so you can tell me what the hell is eating you before I get out of here." He kept his voice low and gave her no chance to respond.

Confused about pretty much everything at the moment, Claire decided that following his instructions was simpler than moderating the debate going on in her mind.

Rosalind was smashing the bananas instead of eating them, and Will was reluctant to have dinner without his mother now that she was home, so she set a place for herself and said she'd be back in a minute.

In the living room, Fletcher didn't even wait for her to say boo before he leveled her with a potent scowl. "What was that damn crap about me saying you're an unfit mother?"

This time, he hadn't lowered his voice at all. Claire regained some of her lost equilibrium by clinging to the morals that had provided her sense of security for years. "Please do not swear in my house."

She crossed her arms and raised her chin, for a moment reclaiming the control that kept her from falling apart.

Fletcher stared hard at the small-boned woman whose expression made a corralled bull's look amenable. He'd known instantly that her oven was beyond repair. The home's ancient appliances, olive-green shag carpet and old-lady furniture (the brown-and-orange flowered sofa had spindly wooden legs and a ruffled *skirt,* for God's sake) reconfirmed his impression that she had zero money, zero taste or both—information his conscience did not need.

When Claire's neighbor had asked if he could watch the boys while she went home to prepare for her bunko game, it had been on the tip of Fletcher's tongue to tell her he had a date with the rest of his whiskey bottle and couldn't babysit. He'd even considered phoning Sophie, something he really hadn't wanted to do. But by then he'd realized that the faucet in Claire's bathroom dripped, which had to be costing her on her water bill, so he'd borrowed Mrs. Gould's son's tool kit and tightened the washer. Claire needed new washers throughout the house. Tomorrow he would stop at the hardware store, get the washers and show her how to replace them, so she wouldn't be reliant on plumbers or neighbors for every repair.

"I will try not to swear if you tell me why you're so touchy."

And then he thought he ought to kick himself. "Rosalind. She looks a lot better, but is she—"

"She'll be fine. She needed an antibiotic. And some Tylenol."

He nodded slowly. "I bought the meals because I figured you wouldn't have a way to cook tonight, and—"

And because he'd still felt guilty about the way he'd treated her when she'd shown up at his house this morning.

It was time for him to go. Time to concentrate on his messed-up, perplexing life, not hers, and to start fixing things more to his liking. Situations were easier to deal with than people. Maybe he'd better not go to the hardware store for her, after all. Probably they'd both be better off if he let her figure out the washers on her own.

Telling himself to be grateful this damned day was almost over, he stalked to the coat tree and lifted his jacket. One arm was shoved through, the second almost there when Claire blurted, "I'm sorry for what I said about the...bottle of alcohol. That was none of my business."

Decent Ms. Dobbs. She'd spoken as if the words had a conscience of their own and needed to come out despite her desire not to talk to him anymore.

"It's your business if I'm watching your kids," he stated, quickly shoving his other arm into the coat.

There was silence. She looked at him in that composed way she had—the Queen of England in a faded dress and cheap shoes. Behind the hazel eyes, however, her emotions were obviously fired up. Her body quivered like a bottle rocket with the fuse lit, and it occurred to him that the widow Dobbs would be a surprise if someone really got to know her.

Fletcher took two big steps to the door. His hand was on the knob—he'd even started to turn it.

"I'm fixing my fencing tomorrow. I'll be out all day. You can use my oven."

Surprise then confusion puckered her delicate features. "What for?"

"To bake the cakes for the bar and grill!" he snapped. Without waiting for a reply, he added, "I'll leave the front door unlocked."

Claire watched Fletcher close the door firmly behind him. What was the man's problem? He changed moods faster than a chameleon changed color. Even though she was off-kilter tonight, she generally stayed pretty even tempered. It was just circumstances and...and *him* that riled her.

Grabbing the little jacket she'd peeled off Rosalind earlier, she carried it to the coat rack and jammed it on the peg Fletcher had just freed. The man clearly had not wanted to offer her the use of his kitchen, so why had he?

"Pity, that's why," she sneered, deciding to open the door and shout after him that she'd rather bake her cakes on a rock in the desert than borrow his oven for a day.

The steam went out of her before she reached for the knob.

She had known Fletcher Kingsley only one day, and although she couldn't be said to have extensive experience with men of his type, she knew already that pity would not motivate him.

Crossing to the sofa, she sat, her hands folded between her knees as she curled forward and rocked, seeking some comfort in a life that was becoming increasingly bumpy.

In the end, it didn't matter why Fletcher had offered her his kitchen; if Bum didn't let her use the restaurant, she would have to take Fletcher up on it.

Rising abruptly, she started toward the kitchen, determined to put the day's worries aside for the rest of the night. On her way, she brushed by the fireplace mantel, and her eyes caught the photo of Arlo on his first fishing trip with Will and Orlie. Her three men stood with their catch, showing it off for the photo. Arlo looked just as proud and happy as their sons. Claire let her fingers trail across the glass protecting the picture. If she'd been a child bride, Arlo had been her child husband. They'd grown up together, trying to create the happiness and security they'd missed in their early lives.

"I'm afraid."

The words slipped out before she could stop them. Before she'd even had a chance to think them, it seemed.

When Arlo died, she'd told herself to *act*, not think, and for almost a year she'd been able to do it. But how much longer could she pretend she was making her life work?

Sliding slowly off the glass, her fingertips curled into a fist. She had spent over half her life refusing to fall apart; she wouldn't give in now.

Deep down, Claire Brewster Dobbs had always known there was no savior for her; if she needed rescuing, she would have to do the job herself.

But as she stood at the fireplace a strange, uncomfortable heat bubbled in her veins. Even though she'd suspected Fletcher of criticizing her competence as a mother, and even though in the dining room she'd gotten angrier with him than she'd gotten with anyone else in years, she had felt relieved, also, by his presence. For the first time in a very long while, with Fletcher in the house, she had stopped feeling alone.

## Chapter Seven

"I know I'm asking too much of you, Irene. And I can't even pay you properly—"

"Psshht! Stop that." Irene Gould stood on Claire's concrete front porch and waved away the apology she neither wanted nor needed. "I couldn't take money today if I wanted it, sweetie girl. It's shabbat, the Jewish Sabbath. If I had grandchildren, I'd be spending time with them today. This is the next best thing." She cuddled Rosalind close to her slight bosom, and the baby babbled happily, her chubby fingers examining Irene's bead necklace.

Seeing her daughter's comfort with their next-door neighbor, Claire knew she ought to feel more grateful than stressed-out today, but no matter what Irene said, she wished fervently she could pay the kind woman in something more than muffins. When she said so, Irene gave her a dismissive wave.

"Your desserts are the best that's happened to me since 1969—and don't ask what happened then, because it's a secret." She tossed her head back to laugh, and Rosalind, who continued to respond wonderfully to the antibiotic and the Tylenol, laughed with her. "You know, before you moved in here, I used to buy all my baked goods from Henry, over at Honey Bea's. He and Miriam, his wife, may her memory be a blessing, owned that place since Henry's father died, back in the sixties. Bea was Henry's mother, and she was a good baker, so when Henry and Miriam took over they used all of Bea's recipes. The results weren't quite the same, but Miriam practiced hard, and she got pretty good. Since she passed away, though—" Irene shook her head gravely "—*oy vey is mir.* Last week, I told him to make me a dozen cream-cheese Danishes for my bridge game. Henry forgot the cream cheese. It was just dough with big empty craters."

"I applied for a job at the bakery as soon as I got to town." Claire reached over with a tissue to give Rosalind's nose a final swipe as she spoke. "Mr. Berns told me he wasn't hiring."

She hadn't meant for the comment to be anything other than conversational, but Irene's expression turned stormy. "That's just like him. Stubborn as a mule! He's waiting for one of his kids to take the business."

"And they won't?"

"He's got one son who's a pediatrician in Portland and another who moved to Los Angeles to make movies. You think either of them is going to come back to Honeyford to knead pumpernickel rolls?" She jiggled the baby and made comforting shushing sounds then continued in a lower voice, "If that stubborn goat keeps this up, half the town will be wearing dentures from biting into his challah."

"Maybe he'll change his mind," Claire said, thinking she'd pay Honey Bea's another visit and talk her way into a job, but Irene's next words dashed any hope that the bakery would be her salvation.

"A zebra changes his stripes more than Henry Berns changes his mind. As long as he can take a breath, he'll do things exactly the way he's always done them." Behind purple-framed glasses, Irene's blue eyes grew teary. Surprised, Claire started to speak, but Irene shook her head vigorously, relieving herself of the sudden emotion. She half shuddered, half shivered. "It's cold out here, and I'm holding you up."

Accepting that the woman did not want to discuss her feelings about the baker, Claire nodded. "It's a nice day, but Rozzy is probably better off inside until it warms up. Thank you again, so much. And don't worry about the boys. As long as they can play in the backyard, they'll be fine."

"I'm not worried, *bubelah*. The boys love it at my house. Good luck today."

Claire kissed Rosalind goodbye, grateful her daughter was so comfortable with someone other than her mother, and watched them head into the house. Irene was becoming like a surrogate grandma to the kids—the kind of relationship Claire had always longed for as a child.

Hefting the tote, laden with baking ingredients, pans and measuring utensils, Claire headed for her Oldsmobile. She'd phoned Bum this morning to see if he'd gotten her note. Though he was sure he'd need additional desserts this weekend, he'd said no to her working in his kitchen. As for in-house employment, she was welcome to fill out an application, but he hadn't hired a new waitress in years.

Loading her supplies in the car, Claire slid behind the wheel, and started the engine. Irene lived with her nephew and his wife and wasn't able to offer the use of an oven, either, so she only hoped Fletcher Kingsley meant what he'd said yesterday when he'd told her she could invade his kitchen.

Because she preferred not to rehash their encounter yesterday evening, she hoped, too, that he'd been honest about having to spend the day outside, mending his fencing. She intended to use his kitchen to bake as many things as she could. Stocking her freezer would allow her to continue peddling her wares around town until she could find a more permanent and lucrative job. Undoubtedly almost anything would be more lucrative than pulling a rolling bakery along in a Radio Flyer wagon and trying to convince shopkeepers to take a coffee break, but something was better than absolutely nothing at all.

Fletcher hadn't given her permission to do more than bake a couple of cakes, and she knew she was taking advantage of his generosity, but the desperation she'd been beating back for months rose like lava.

Rozzy and even Orlando were still happily unaware of the uncertainty in which their small family lived. But every time Claire looked into William's eyes…

She pulled out of the driveway a bit too quickly, spinning fine gravel into the air, and had to remind herself to take her foot off the gas. It was in Will's nature to worry, but he had no way of knowing what kind of insecurity they truly faced, or what could happen to a family when Daddy had never gotten around to buying a life insurance policy and Mama hadn't graduated from high school.

Self-recrimination filled Claire's mouth like bile. That kind of regret could reduce a person to tears or give her a spine of steel. She chose steel.

Fletcher slapped his Stetson against his thigh as he limped across the length of his brother's living room. When he reached the wall with a framed black-and-white photo of the building in which he currently paced, he turned, slapped his thigh harder and limped the other way. He had just dug his cell phone from his pocket and started to thumb in numbers when the front door, leading up from the pharmacy, opened.

"About damn time!" He flipped the cell phone shut. "I haven't got all day to wait for you. What the hell took so long?"

"Wow." Garbed in the white lab coat that was destined to make Fletcher think of a laundry commercial every time he saw it, Dean placed an expressive hand on his chest. "Man, I am sorry. I should have considered your schedule when you phoned me from my apartment to tell me I had to leave work and meet you up here *right away*." He tossed a set of keys into a square dish that sat in the middle of a long narrow table behind the couch. "Damn, I'm selfish."

Fletcher refused to be cowed. "It's noon. You take a lunch break, don't you?"

"I eat standing up." Shrugging out of the lab coat and laying it neatly over the back of the leather sofa, rather than tossing it as Fletcher would have, Dean loosened the buttons of his cuffs and rolled up his sleeves as he walked to the kitchen. "How'd you get in here, anyway?"

"Jimmied the lock. You need a dead bolt. The world's no longer a safe place, or hadn't you heard?" He followed his brother into the short L-shaped kitchen.

"So we're having a good morning?" Dean spoke in the perennially tolerant tone that was guaranteed to bug lesser mortals.

"It's a swell day in the neighborhood, Mr. Rogers. Look, I want to talk to you fast and then I've got things to do."

Dean opened the sleek black refrigerator to withdraw a loaf of dark bread, a container of turkey, a jar of tiny fancy-looking pickles and lite mayo—*lite,* for God's sake. Fletcher shook his head. "You can take the boy out of the city."

Dean returned a bland smile. "What do you want on your sandwich?"

Surprised, although he knew he shouldn't be—Dean had always had perfect manners—Fletcher moved closer to examine the food laid on the dark granite counter. "What kind of bread is that?"

"It's made from sprouted wheat berries. The new doctor in town is a big fan of flourless products. She managed to get both markets to stock them, then convinced me it was my civic duty to buy a loaf."

Fletcher frowned in distaste at the grainy, seed-studded bread. "It looks like it was made by a constipated canary." Dean winced at the crude description, which made Fletcher smile inside. "You have any cheese?"

Placing a package of sliced Muenster on the counter, Dean started to assemble a sandwich, but Fletcher waved away the effort. "Just the cheese."

He reached over, helped himself to three slices that were stuck together and took a large bite since he'd missed breakfast. Before he could get down to business so he could get out of here, Dean asked, "How are your cholesterol levels?"

Taking his cheese to the opposite counter, Fletcher leaned back and tilted his head, openly assessing his only remaining blood relation. "I see why you never bothered to marry. You're already your own wife."

Seemingly immune to Fletcher's other jibes, Dean nevertheless frowned at that one. If Fletcher didn't know better, he'd have thought he'd actually hurt his brother's feelings. Fortunately Deano had always lived as if he carried a leveler in his hip pocket: listing slightly in one moment, he managed to even himself out in the next.

Fletcher took another bite of the Muenster, but it was tasteless now. He began to feel the walls of the small kitchen closing in on him. Dean had made significant cosmetic changes to the interior of the apartment, but in Fletcher's eyes, the old walls still sagged with the weight of the secrets they knew.

"Let's get down to business," he said, eschewing niceties since he was about to do something he loathed in front of the person he most loathed doing it with. It took a couple of tries before he unlocked his jaw enough to push out the words. "I need a favor."

Dutch apple, pumpkin and lemon-custard pies cooled on the kitchen counter. The layers for Claire's special mile-high fudge cake rose obediently in the oven, and a double batch of oatmeal chocolate-chip cookies waited their turn.

Giving a last brisk whipping to a bowl of frosting, Claire set it aside, then let her tense shoulders droop a minute and stretched to work a kink from her back. If she sold everything she'd just made, she might have enough money to buy food for the week without wiping out the remainder of her bank account, but that wasn't good enough. If they had another emergency like yesterday's, they'd be ruined.

"Sailor muffins," she said beneath her breath, thinking she could quite possibly sell them to the staff at the boys' school on Monday morning. Wondering if she had enough powdered sugar left for the glaze, she decided to take a quick bathroom break before she got started.

Her stomach growled insistently as she walked through a narrow hallway that formed the main artery of the long house. Fletcher had left the front door open, as promised, and though she'd been here for almost three hours, she hadn't seen a sign of him.

At one point she'd opened the refrigerator to store the milk she'd brought with her and had seen with some surprise that he had nothing to eat except some eggs. That was it. There wasn't even butter to fry them in. Unable to quell her curiosity, she told herself that looking in a cupboard when you had permission to use someone's kitchen wasn't *exactly* snooping.

There were a couple of dishes in the upper cabinets, a skillet and small pot below the stove and a few boxes of food in the pantry—two kinds of cereal that were going to go down hard without milk, a box of crackers as yet unopened, and a can of chili. There wasn't a fruit or vegetable in sight and nothing, really, to indicate that this kitchen served a *home*.

Questions and even a surge of compassion had swelled in Claire when she'd made her discovery, but she'd known absolutely that Fletcher Kingsley would not welcome her sympathy. He'd bristle like a porcupine if she showed any undue interest in his life. So, she'd made her mind switch channels by mentally calculating the profits of what she'd baked up to that point.

Unfortunately as she walked down the hall on her way to the bathroom, her curiosity began to poke at her again. Dull beige wallpaper with faded gold stripes covered the walls, and a few wobbly picture hooks hung uselessly from skinny nails. In square footage, this house was bigger than anyplace Claire had ever lived, or ever hoped to. Yet it looked old and unloved and generally gave off a feeling of impermanence.

Aunt Faylene's furnishings were old, and Claire wasn't tasteless enough not to realize the house cried "old lady" the minute you walked into it, but there was a sweet comfort to the shabbiness. The house had been lived in, laughed in. Loved in.

If Fletcher Kingsley's place could talk, it would grumble, "Get the *bleep* out."

In the hall bathroom, Claire found further evidence of Fletcher's disinterest in domestic details. The plastic shower curtain was patterned with pineapples and tiny palm trees, many of them rubbed off by time. There was no way he'd chosen that curtain, but neither had he bothered to replace it. Over the aged porcelain sink, the light fixture was practically crying for someone to take steel wool to its chrome base to remove the rust that had settled there.

Fletcher hadn't even thought to hang a hand towel. Claire told herself to be grateful there was toilet paper.

Then, as she started to leave, her eye caught sight of something surprising. A bit of decorating that could only have come from him.

Above the toilet—the toilet, for heaven's sake—was a framed, velvet-backed display of four large belt buckles. Claire may never have cared much about rodeo, but she could see that the buckles were awards. Fletcher had won national rodeo championships at least four times. She leaned close to examine the glass-covered prizes.

She'd heard of actors putting Oscar statuettes in their bathrooms, but that seemed sort of ironic and deliberately humble. And, she bet the bathrooms had marble counters, real crystal fixtures and hand towels.

Fletcher's decorating choice seemed to overshoot irony, landing more in the vicinity of disrespect.

Without being sure quite why, Claire felt sparks of irritation, like pricks of static electricity, when she imagined him setting something he ought to be grateful for in this dingy bathroom.

Managing time well was one of her gifts, and she'd had a good work ethic even when she'd been a stay-at-home mother. But rather than returning to the kitchen to start on her muffins, she let her interest lead her down the hallway in the opposite direction from the kitchen. There were a number of bedrooms into which she poked her nosy head, shutting the doors again as soon as she ascertained that nothing personal lurked in the rooms' darkened interiors—not even beds. Finally, at the end of the hall, behind a painted wooden door, she found a room with a king-sized bed, an end table with a simple lamp and several cardboard boxes stacked against the wall beneath the window. Rumpled sheets covered the unmade mattress, and the sliding mirrored door to the closet sat open to reveal a dozen shirts along with several pairs of jeans on hangers. Cowboy hats very neatly lined the shelf above the clothes rods.

Fletcher's bedroom.

*Alrighty, time to get back to work.* It was just as plain as day that she absolutely, positively had no business in this room. Never mind that a pile of magazines sat on the top box and that she found herself wondering whether his choice of reading materials would impart some insight into how he could go from hot to cold faster than a frog ate flies. There was right and there was wrong, and the space in between wasn't all that wide.

Claire's stomach rumbled, and she figured she'd just head back to the kitchen and eat the peanut butter sandwich she'd brought from home….

And maybe have a glass of the milk she'd brought to thin the frosting…

And then she could start on those muffins…

By the time she thought the word "muffin," she was all the way in the room, her hand reaching toward the top magazine on the stack.

Fifteen minutes later, she was on the phone to Irene.

"Tell me everything you know about Fletcher Kingsley."

Something chocolate.

In a house that, for two weeks, had generated no aroma more appealing than a microwaved frozen dinner, the fragrant blend of butter and sugar, cocoa and cinnamon, came as a surprise, even though Fletcher had known Claire would be baking in his kitchen today. He'd stayed away until late afternoon, giving her plenty of time to do her business and scram before his return.

So what was her car doing in the arc of his circular driveway?

He'd considered pulling away when he saw the car and giving her more time, but the bed of his truck was loaded with supplies he wanted to unload before dark. And, unwilling to socialize at one of the local eateries, he'd stopped by the market to pick up frozen enchiladas. But he walked into the house, the thought of eating anything made in a factory rapidly lost its appeal.

Something had happened to his kitchen.

A display of pies, cookies, muffins and fudge-frosted chocolate cakes too high to be real snaked across the counter like a jewel-studded necklace. The coffee-maker carafe was filled to the brim, and the orange light was on, signaling that the coffee was fresh.

Sink, countertops and floors had been wiped so clean they sparkled despite their age, and damned if he couldn't hear Frank Sinatra promising to be home for Christmas.

The music was coming from the living room. Fletcher looked for a place to set his small bag of groceries then walked slowly toward the living room, his boots sounding heavy on the linoleum and his palms sweating, though he had no idea why.

He moved through the short hallway and into a living area whose brown carpet appeared warm rather than dingy in the glow of a blaze that crackled in the fireplace. The furniture he'd dumped into the space had been arranged more invitingly and...what the hell? A copy of *PSN Rodeo* magazine lay angled on the coffee table.

"You're back. Hi."

His head whipped around. Claire entered from the hallway, a rag in one hand and a bottle of cleaning solution in the other. She'd gathered her hair on top of her head, but a few thick locks had fallen free. She wore jeans today, topped by a pale pink blouse that hugged her generous bosom. Her cheeks glowed from exertion and the firelight.

Fletcher swallowed hard. This wasn't what he'd expected when he'd walked in the door. And it wasn't what he wanted. Letting her use the house was meant to end their exchange, not continue it.

"What do you think you're doing?" The words sounded harsh and demanding.

Blinking hazel eyes registered his anger, but if he expected Claire to quail, he got a second surprise. She smiled like Martha Stewart being paid a compliment on her domestic skills.

"This is a great house. All it needs is some elbow grease to make it livable. It feels a lot better already, doesn't it?"

The fire spit and crackled.

"Where did you get the logs?" Fletcher demanded. He hadn't split any wood yet. A closer look told him she'd purchased an overpriced pressed log, or had given him one intended for her family.

"There's nothing like a fire in the evening, is there? If you're hungry, I've got cookies and coffee in the kitchen. Or help yourself to a muffin. I made an extra batch to leave with you."

A cauldron of emotion burned inside Fletcher, thick as lava, making it impossible to speak. Claire hesitated then plowed ahead with the-show-must-go-on enthusiasm. "Sailor muffins, they're called. They're real hearty and sweet. And they'd be just delicious with eggs and sausage in the morning."

He took a menacing step toward the woman who in two short days had barged into his life without permission. He didn't want whatever she was selling—or the feelings she was awakening in him.

"I don't want a muffin. Not one. Not a batch." When the first step put a flicker of uncertainty in her eyes, he took another. "I don't give a damn how good they are." Before he could tell her the party was over and she had to leave, his attention was caught by the reflection of flickering flames. He looked up.

Above the sofa, nestled on black velvet and encased in a custom mahogany frame studded with carved horseshoes, his first four rodeo championship buckles winked at him from the wall. He'd framed them as ornately as he could, imagining his father seeing them someday, believing the success of a son who had been expected to land in jail would somehow force Victor to acknowledge his own failure as a husband and father.

Unfortunately, Fletcher never had gotten around to shoving his success in Victor's face. For years, he hadn't wanted to return to Honeyford, so he'd waited for his moment, amassing as many wins and as much trophy money as he could. A few years back, after a particularly big championship, he'd received a brief letter of congratulations from his father. *"Dean tells me you won a couple of buckles in the Wrangler Tour. Congratulations."*

A couple of buckles. He had broken records in a competition that had spanned seven months. In rodeo after rodeo, he had stayed the course, hung on to bulls and broncs that had seemed intent on murder. Fletcher had never backed down.

*I learned not to break from you, Dad.* That was what he'd wanted to tell Victor, though he wouldn't have meant it as a compliment. He'd never gotten the chance. At the height of Fletcher's success, Victor had had the gall to die.

"I put those in the bathroom," Fletcher growled now, jerking his head toward the framed buckles.

Claire nodded. She still wasn't going to back down, he could see that, but for once her expressive face closed up like a clam. "They shouldn't be there. They look like something to be proud of. And this room needed something to make it more personal."

"I'll be damned if I remember asking you to comment on the décor. I said you could use the kitchen."

"Which I appreciate very much. I can't offer you any money as thanks, so I cleaned up a little."

"I didn't ask for money. Or thanks." Trying to control a response that felt explosive, almost violent in its intensity, he stepped away from her and assessed the room. "You did more than clean up." Picking a magazine off the coffee table, he saw that it was an issue of *PSN* with him on the cover. He wanted to crumple the magazine. He wanted to douse the warmth emanating from the hearth and undo every change she'd made.

Fletcher hadn't felt warm in this room since he had been eight years old. Any time he'd thought of the ranch house in the years he'd been away, he'd felt a desire to possess it, but never had he imagined it could feel like home again. There had been no reason to believe the feeling of home would come again ever, anywhere, and he'd long ago stopped yearning. Until he'd walked into the kitchen tonight.

For a moment, he'd felt the presence of something alive and clean and pure. In that unguarded gap of time, Claire Dobbs had infused light into the darkness it had taken him years to accept.

Instead of giving him comfort, her meddling ignited the urge to strike out. Beneath that impulse anger and panic surged. For a second, Fletcher felt almost blind with it, and he began to sweat. A film of perspiration covered his face, and suddenly he understood.

Fueling his discomfort, feeding the sense of urgency and the rage, lurked the most dangerous feeling of all, the one he could not stand and refused to entertain again in this disappointment-packed life: hope.

## *Chapter Eight*

Despite a pounding heart and cheeks buzzing with heat, Claire knew she had to stand her ground. What choice did she have? As soon as she'd seen those rodeo magazines, with Fletcher on the cover of nearly every one, she'd known the answer to her family's dilemma was at her fingertips. Irene Gould hadn't lived in Honeyford while Fletcher was growing up, but she'd heard that his career had made him a very wealthy man and told Claire, too, that Fletcher appeared in magazine ads and even a TV commercial. That was all Claire needed to know.

She had enough money to pay perhaps one utility bill this month and to buy food for the next two weeks. Period. Then she could peddle cinnamon buns up one side of Main Street and down another, and it wouldn't save her.

For years she'd successfully wiped away the pain of her own youth, but the eraser she'd used was the faith that her children would never know such uncertainty. That faith was gone now, leaving fear in its wake.

Smiling required a Herculean effort. Looking into Fletcher Kingsley's stormy face, she did it, anyway. Real, real big.

"Doing all the outside work around the ranch is bound to take up most of your day. It makes sense that you wouldn't have time to think about fixing up the house or stocking the kitchen or making a home-cooked meal." While she'd frosted her cakes and filled muffin cups, she'd thought about what she was going to say, and she was darn well going to get it out, every last word, even with Fletcher's eyebrows lowering a bit more on each syllable.

It had taken years for the Department of Human Services to discover that Claire's mother was incapable of providing a proper home. Then a social worker had arrived at her school one day, and she'd been taken to a foster family, where a trash bag stuffed with her clothes and a single book became her only link to anything familiar.

What if it didn't take Child Welfare as long this time to discover that the apple hadn't fallen very far from the tree? What if she couldn't pay for heat or electricity, and the boys mentioned it at school, and someone reported her?

Fear surged into her throat; purpose pushed it down again. Fletcher Kingsley needed the services she could provide, he had the money to pay her for them, and he was damn well going to listen to her.

"A man trying to establish himself in a town needs a house that looks well kept. And you can't eat out for every meal, because it's not practical. Also it's not good for your health or your budget."

Fletcher ran a shaking hand through his hair, muttering angrily under his breath.

"If you're upset about the buckles, I won't move anything else. It's just that there wasn't much here to decorate with,

,o—" The look on his face stopped her. "Never mind decorating." Changing tack, she spoke quickly. "I can cook for you, and keep this house spotless. I know how to do yard work and small repairs, too. I could put a garden around the house. It would make the front door look more inviting. And if you're having guests for Thanksgiving, I'd be happy to make the dinner for no extra charge, above and beyond my agreed-on salary."

Lips compressed, Fletcher took a noisy breath in and out of his nose. Tension buzzed along his jaw line. There seemed to be an excess of energy inside him, though on the surface he remained almost unnaturally still.

"I'll work harder than any three people," Claire persisted, knowing she had only one shot at convincing him. "You won't hear me complain about the hours, and I'm healthy as a horse. I won't miss work. The only family I've got is my kids, and they're young yet, so if you need me to work Christmas, too…" She hesitated only a second. "I can do that. I can. No problem."

Fletcher closed his eyes. When he opened them again, the yellow glow from the lamp on the end table imparted an eerie flame to ebony pupils. His hushed voice throbbed with opposition.

"You'd work for me, a man you don't know, alone in my house? We're miles out of town, sweetheart. Who's going to hear you if I get out of hand?"

Adrenaline rushed through Claire. She told herself it was due to surprise rather than fear. "You're just trying to scare me."

"Wrong. I *am* scary."

"I don't believe you."

She didn't know for sure whether to believe him or not, but she thought she saw a flicker of uncertainty in his eyes. Coupled with her own desperation, it was enough to make her stay the course. When Fletcher growled, "You don't want to work for me," she didn't even hesitate.

"Yes, I do. You need help around here, and I'm applying. I'm the best you're going to get, Mr. Kingsley. I'll work on a straight salary and give you free overtime. And I'll shop for you when I get my own groceries, so you won't have to pay me for that. I can even run errands *after* work." She began to count on her fingers all the great perks he'd be getting by hiring her. "That's cooking, cleaning, yard work, shopping, preparation of holiday meals and unpaid errands. You won't get a better deal anywhere."

With every point she made, Claire imagined Fletcher softening until he admitted she was exactly what he needed. One careful glance at his expression disabused her of that hope.

His lips parted, grim and unpleasant in a poor facsimile of a smile, and he took another step forward. Involuntarily, Claire backed up, but the corner of the end table stopped her. Fletcher advanced until he was so close she felt his breath on her cheek. The hair on the back of her neck tickled.

"You have no idea what I need." His voice sounded like wheels on gravel. "In fact, you left out about the only thing I *do* want from a woman."

His gaze lowered to her bosom, but only for a second. As soon as he realized where his attention drifted, he jerked it back to her face. Claire watched his expression go from menacing to hungry to, if she looked deeply enough, uncertain. Fear of him melted, replaced by awareness—the awareness of his physical attraction to her, and of the warmth stealing through her own body. Time grew blurry as senses sharpened, and her desperation to secure a job turned into distant thunder.

Uncertain of exactly when he took hold of her shoulders, Claire did not resist as Fletcher pressed his mouth to hers. She felt a day's growth of beard and lips that were hard and

▼ If offer card is missing write to: The Reader Service, P.O. Box 1867, Buffalo, NY 14240-1867 or visit www.ReaderService.com ▼

# Send For
# 2 FREE BOOKS
## Today!

## I accept your offer!

Please send me two free
Silhouette Special Edition®
novels and two mystery
gifts (gifts worth about $10).
I understand that these books
are completely free—even
the shipping and handling will
be paid—and I am under no
obligation to purchase anything, ever,
as explained on the back of this card.

**About how many NEW paperback fiction books have you purchased in the past 3 months?**

| ❑ 0-2 | ❑ 3-6 | ❑ 7 or more |
|-------|-------|-------------|
| E7NV  | E7N7  | E7PK        |

235/335 SDL

*Please Print*

FIRST NAME

LAST NAME

ADDRESS

APT.#                CITY

Visit us online at
www.ReaderService.com

STATE/PROV.          ZIP/POSTAL CODE

unyielding, his mind obviously resisting the seduction his body urged. Then abruptly his lips softened. Claire raised her arms, her fingers reaching to touch his face, but before she made contact, he jumped back as if she were a flame and he a hollow log. The kiss ended as quickly as it had begun, and Claire was grateful for the table behind her; her boneless legs felt too weak to stand.

A thousand hooves stampeded over her heart. The air seemed to have been compressed from her lungs, and for a second she felt panicked, the way she did when she contemplated her future. Her chest and face flamed.

Through the buzzing confusion in her ears, one thought emerged: he was more frightened than she.

Pulling the courage up from her feet, she looked him in the eye. "So, is that a yes then?"

If she achieved nothing else here today, at least she had temporarily stunned Fletcher. His brows dipped lower, looking as if someone had tattooed a hawk in flight over his eyes.

"No," he ground out. "It is not. Go, Claire. Get your cakes and your pies and get out. You're barking up the wrong tree here. I don't like sweets."

While Claire collected her things from his kitchen, Fletcher hid out in the bedroom, every muscle bunching against the urge to pace, his fists clenching and unclenching.

He'd never needed a woman out of his life as much as he needed this one out.

Crossing to the double windows, which overlooked the driveway, he remembered when flowers had lined the walkway to the porch and spilled from baskets hanging in the portico, even in winter. His mother, Jule, had liked color everywhere.

This ranch had been in Jule's family for three generations.

Fletcher remembered his young mother as vivacious, endlessly fun, perpetually young. She'd taught him to play waterballoon basketball. When Victor had been out of town, she'd awakened Fletcher at midnight and led him to the kitchen, where a grand display of his favorite junk foods had awaited him on the kitchen table. She'd ridden her horse bareback and occasionally without a bridle as well, claiming she could control her mount with her thoughts.

Life with Jule had been punctuated by laughter and loud music, acceptance and noisy joy. On the good days.

On the not-so-good days, she had cloistered herself in the bedroom she'd shared with Victor. During those darker times, Fletcher's grandfather, who had still owned the place and with whom they'd all lived, would try to keep Fletcher working on the ranch, away from the house, but usually not before Fletcher had heard the shouting between his mother and father, the items thrown against a wall, the muted sobbing.

Victor had never enjoyed living on the ranch, nor had he appreciated his wife's ebullient nature. Widowed and taking care of Dean by himself when he'd met the much younger Jule, Victor had, as far as Fletcher could tell, scored a mother for his firstborn son and then tried to crush all the life out of her in order to make her fit his perception of the respectable, small-town doctor's wife.

Eventually Victor had insisted they move off the ranch and into town, a decision that had seemed to change Jule profoundly. Young, idiosyncratic and free-spirited, she couldn't meet the conservative community's expectations. She never fit in, a situation that had caused her great pain and Victor much embarrassment. Eventually, after Jule had grown miserable enough, Victor had allowed mother and son to return to the ranch, while he remained in town with Dean, but Jule had never recaptured her joy. Loving a man who hadn't deserved it, she'd tormented herself over Victor's disapproval.

Watching his beloved mother suffer, Fletcher had made his way to Victor's apartment in town, hoping to convince his father to move back to the ranch and to make Jule happy again. The attempt had backfired horribly.

Rubbing his face as if he could wipe away the memories, Fletcher wondered if he would ever find solace on this ranch again then reminded himself that solace was not his goal. He wanted to turn this place that his father had loathed and his mother had loved, this land that held the memory of their laughter and their joy, into the biggest and best ranch in the area. He wanted to rub the success of it into the faces of everyone who had supported Victor and disrespected his mother.

Placing his fists on the windowpane, he gazed at the front of the property, at the long stately driveway that led to the house and the circular drive intended to accommodate a bevy of cars, but where only two vehicles currently parked—Fletcher's four-by-four and Claire's ancient sedan.

Claire was an obstacle he could not hazard. He stared at the dull green of the Oldsmobile that should have been retired to the scrap heap a good decade ago. The body of the vinyl-roofed workhorse was remarkably free of dents, but rust pocked every piece of visible chrome.

Fletcher had a lot in common with that car—they were both so battered by the roads they'd traveled that nothing was going to fix them. Yet Claire probably told her children the old beater was a chariot and made them believe it. If he let her, she would try to make him believe there was still some shine left on him, too.

Already aware of Claire's innate integrity and tenderness, he continued to be blindsided by her grit. A hundred years ago, he and his mother had watched an old movie starring Debbie Reynolds. *The Unsinkable Molly Brown*. Jule had gotten so caught up in the movie, she'd had a T-shirt made with Molly Brown's trademark slogan "I ain't down yet!" and had danced around in it every day for a week. Then the T-shirt had disappeared, and, come to think of it, Fletcher had never seen it again.

Why had he thought of that now?

*Because Claire won't sink.*

The thought came to him as the woman walked down his porch steps, lugging three canvas totes stuffed, he assumed, with baked goods. His mother had been emotionally fragile, easy to break. He remembered feeling the need to shelter her, to protect Jule from the world when he was no older than Will Dobbs.

Claire was different. She stood on two strong legs. He couldn't see her expression from here, but watched her load the car then return to the house and emerge a couple of minutes later with her arms full of plastic containers. Loading those, too, into the low-riding sedan, she got into the car without glancing again at the house. The fact that he wished she had looked up merely reinforced what he'd realized when he'd kissed her.

She'd been dead-on right when she'd accused him of trying to scare her; he'd wanted her to run from him. Unfortunately he'd jolted himself more than her. Sometime during that kiss—which had probably lasted a few seconds, but had felt like eternity—he had come into contact with a piece of his soul that had not completely died.

And that was unacceptable.

The Oldsmobile's tires spit gravel as Claire drove away, and Fletcher tried not to think about whether she was riding on bald tires or whether she knew how to examine them. He'd tell his do-gooder brother to check out the tires, and he'd insist that Dean find a job to give Claire. Dean would do it, because getting involved was his M.O.

Employed, Claire would have the income to take care of

her family's basic needs, and Fletcher wouldn't have to see her anymore. Or to wonder how so much desperation and so much faith could possibly exist in one person's eyes.

Then, if he wasn't worrying about her, he could quite possibly forget that before he'd ended their kiss he had imagined—just for a second—giving in to the demands of his father's will. And that as he had envisioned marrying to inherit his ranch, the wife he had pictured was Claire.

"Oh, dear lord. I have got to stop buying your muffins." Gabriella Coombs, owner and proprietor of the Honey Comb Barbershop on Third Street, squeezed her hands together under her chin, as if she were trying to keep her plump fingers from snatching one of the delectable treats in Claire's basket. "Ooh, I want you and you and you and you," she said to the muffins, cookies and cinnamon rolls tucked into the napkin-lined wicker.

Claire had immediately frozen a good portion of the food she'd made at Fletcher's house then took everything out of the freezer last night, sprinkled the muffins and cinnamon rolls with water and steamed them back to freshness on this Monday morning.

"The pumpkin muffins are low fat. I substituted applesauce for half the oil," she said, smiling at Gabby, whose barbershop had become one of Claire's regular stops when she made her rounds through town, selling her baked goods and sandwiches from the Radio Flyer wagon she'd parked out front.

Ordinarily, one of the two barber chairs was full when Claire came in and there were at least two men waiting. This morning the place was empty.

"Maybe I'll get a cinnamon roll," Gabby said, her pretty gray-blue eyes widening as she contemplated the calorie count. "That's probably all my Weight Watchers points until 2012, but oh, well."

Plucking a sweet cinnamon-stuffed bun with thick icing from the basket, she smelled it first, humming her pleasure before she took a big, sensuous bite. "Mmmm. Ohhhh. Claire, you are a miracle worker. Wars would end if governments could taste your baking. Do you have a whole pie? I'm going to my parents' tonight for dinner."

"I have a lemon custard."

"Sold." Setting the cinnamon roll atop on an orange flyer announcing Honeyford's Halloween parade, Gabby brushed her hands and said, "Let me get your cash."

Claire followed her to the old-fashioned register. Sales had been slow this morning, and she fretted over having defrosted everything she'd baked this weekend. With her oven still on the fritz she didn't know when she'd have another opportunity to bake.

Since Saturday, all she'd thought about was how to get steady employment…when she wasn't thinking about Fletcher, his kiss and the lies he was telling.

"Oh, nuts. I don't have any petty cash. Honestly, I am so forgetful lately." Gabby shook her head. "I'll run to the back and get my purse."

"All right. While you're doing that, I'll get the pie. I have one in the wagon." Claire headed to the street, grateful for the brief respite so Gabby wouldn't see her face turn red. She'd been blushing a lot this weekend.

Fletcher's kiss had sent a ribbon of heat into her belly that returned full force every time she remembered it. He had intended for the kiss to scare her off, of course, but the more she thought about it (and she'd been thinking about it a lot), the more convinced she was that Fletcher was a fraud. He portrayed himself as mean, uncaring and a natural loner, but he had a conscience. He made amends when he was wrong, he cared about children and he was not a man who could comfortably bully a woman. His kiss may have started out fierce, but on the tail end, it had turned unbelievably gentle. Almost…uncertain.

After tossing and turning Saturday night and fretting all day Sunday, Claire had come to the realization that Fletcher Kingsley was frightened of something and didn't want anyone to see it. He blustered and steamed and made himself generally disagreeable to keep people at arm's length.

Setting her basket in the creaky red wagon, Claire removed the pie and carried it to the barbershop. Gabby was still in the back. As Claire waited in front of the register, her gaze rose to a poster she hadn't noticed before. Positioned on the wall directly behind and above the front desk, a large black-and-white picture showed a man and woman laughing with a child, their beautiful heads close together, their hair perfect. The woman's wispy blond, head-hugging style made her look happy, sexy and carefree. Claire felt a pang of envy even though the photo had been staged. Would she feel that carefree again?

*Have you* ever *felt that carefree?*

"Here we go." Gabby bustled back into the room, a wad of small bills in her hand. "I know it's a dollar for the cinnamon roll—which is way too little, Claire, really—but how much for the pie? And don't say anything less than ten dollars, because you can't get an artisan-made pie these days for under twelve."

"Artisan-made?" Claire shrugged. Her attention was still on the photo. "Has that always been here?"

Gabby turned. "The poster? No. They send them sometimes from the product companies. I got that with my last shipment of hair spray. I thought maybe if I put it up, I could make the shop seem more…I don't know…" Her full lips pouted. "Hip or something." She sighed heavily and smacked a few keys on the register. The door dinged as it opened. "Okay, I'm going to give you twelve dollars for the pie, because I know you'll undercut yourself if I let you set the price."

Counting the cash in her hand, she tucked several bills into the register and held the rest out.

Claire started to set the pie on Gabby's chipped marble counter so she could take the money, but her gaze rose again to the photo, and she hesitated.

Happy...carefree...sexy...

All she'd ever asked out of life was to feel safe.

Suddenly the pie felt heavy in her hands. Again she started to set it down. Her eyes met Gabby's, the other woman smiled, and Claire blurted, "Will you trade the pie for a haircut?"

Gabby blinked, caught off guard. "You want a haircut?"

Like a magnet, the poster commanded Claire's gaze. A startling longing rose inside her.

"I want that haircut." She nodded to the woman in the photo. Her palms began to perspire as Gabby glanced over her shoulder.

When the sweet redheaded barber turned back, she looked like Orlando the time he saw his first Ferris wheel—thrilled and reluctant all at once. "You want me to do that? But I cut men's hair."

"Well," Claire cocked her head at the poster, "it's pretty short."

"Yes, but... Oh, Claire. I put up that picture because ever since Delilah bought Helen's Hair Hive, she's taken all my male customers under eighty. That doesn't mean I can actually cut hair like she does." She flapped the hand holding the money. "The truth is that woman has more style in her stiletto than I have in my whole body. If you want a great cut you should go to her." Sadness filled Gabby's big eyes. "*I'd* go to her, except I'd rather eat rat poison." She reached for the cinnamon roll, took a big bite and sniffled a little as she chewed.

Claire bit her lip before she spoke. "Don't take this the wrong way, Gabby, but Delilah's salon intimidates me. I'm much more comfortable here. And I doubt Delilah would trade a haircut for a pie."

"That's probably true. Unless it's made with Splenda and the crust is spelt." They smiled at each other. Gabby turned again to study the poster. "That would be an adorable style on you. What if I mess it up, though, and—"

"I've worn a ponytail nearly every day since my oldest child was born. Anything you do will be an improvement."

Gabby hesitated a few seconds more then blurted, "Okay. I'll cut your hair." They moved quickly after that, as if time might give them a chance to change their minds.

Within a minute, Claire was seated in the plump, leather-cushioned barber's chair, a black cape tossed over her to protect her clothes. Tucking a paper collar around Claire's neck, Gabby studied her client. With the first *snick* of the scissors, Claire felt her heartbeat pick up.

She knew exactly why she was getting this haircut. Fletcher Kingsley had kissed her, and for the first time in her life, she had felt out of control—and liked it.

Out of control. Sexy. Young. He hadn't meant for her to feel any of those things—she knew that, but had felt them nonetheless.

As Gabby pressed her head forward gently, Claire looked down.

With her gaze on her own lap and the scissors whispering behind her, she thought about Fletcher and Arlo. One man had been as sweet as the custard pie on Gabby's counter. He'd welcomed friends and community into his life; he'd been endlessly accepting. He'd made everything simple.

The other man carried secrets and pains and yearnings he likely didn't admit even to himself. He'd rather be lonely than face all the complexities of life.

After being married to the former man—and loving him—for eight serene years, how was it that Claire felt she understood the latter man so much better? Why were his stormy eyes the ones she imagined widening in surprise, and darkening with pleasure, when she showed off her new haircut?

## Chapter Nine

Gabby used her smallest pair of scissors to take a tiny, final snip from behind Claire's ear. Standing back, she studied her work carefully then nodded. "All right. We're done."

Taking a deep breath, she put a hand on the chair and turned Claire slowly toward the mirror. Clutching comb and scissors in her nervous fists, she shrugged her shoulders. "What do you think?"

The reflection that had greeted Claire for every one of her adult years had shown an ordinary woman, on the plain side, very much someone who looked as if she'd rather read a cookbook than a fashion magazine. That woman was nowhere in sight. With a cap of blond waves cut to just below her ears, Claire looked, finally, like the young woman she was. Beneath the protective cape, her clothes remained more suited to visit the local grocery store than to go clubbing, but from the neck up she looked and, more incredibly, felt ready to jump up and dance.

"Oh, my goodness."

"I know." Gabby breathed the words on a sigh that sounded both relieved and excited. "It's fabulous, isn't it? I can't believe I did it."

Reaching up, Claire touched the blond wisps that teased her cheek as she turned her head from side to side. Her heart fluttered happily. Not a thing had changed in her life—except for the fact that she now had one less pie to sell, which put her one step closer to dead broke—but she felt more hopeful somehow.

Gabby removed the tissue and black cape from around Claire's neck. Together, they walked to the counter. "You need a little makeup now," Gabby said. "I'd help you with that, but I'm hopeless. I buy new makeup every year and just wind up looking like a different kind of clown. Maybe it's my coloring." Picking up her forgotten cinnamon bun, she took a big, happy bite. "I hope you have someplace fun to go today. Somewhere you can be admired," she said, licking the frosting from her lips.

Before Claire could respond that she was going to have to rely on two males under the age of eight to admire her, the door to the barbershop opened, and Gabby, who was still chewing, almost choked.

"Good morning." Dean Kingsley's smooth-as-butter voice carried a smile.

Shoving the remainder of her treat below the counter, Gabby frantically swallowed and wiped her mouth. "Good morning!" She smiled hugely. Her blushing cheeks did, indeed, clash with her red hair. "I don't usually see you here during the day," she told her new arrival. "Do you need a haircut? I mean, you look just fine. But, if you're here for a trim, I could do that. Now." She gestured to the two empty chairs. "I'm free."

Dean shook his head, his calm demeanor a sharp contrast

to Gabby's agitation. "I will come in for a trim, Gabriella, but probably closer to the end of the week. This morning, I stopped in because I saw Claire's wagon out front." He turned to her. "Have you got a minute?"

Claire nodded, noting that Dean completely missed the way Gabby's expression fell or how hard she tried to rally. "Gabby just cut my hair," she told him. "I was so used to my old ponytail, I hardly recognize myself. She certainly is talented."

Dean blinked distractedly. "Oh. Yes. You look lovely." He smiled—gracious, sincere and completely oblivious.

"I'll put this in the fridge," Gabby said disappointedly, plucking the custard pie off the counter. "I'm having dinner with my parents," she explained. "Dad loves custard."

"I haven't seen Frank in a while. How's his hernia?"

Claire winced. Even Arlo, who hadn't known much about flirting, would not have blown the moment so badly. Dean seemed completely unaware of Gabby's very apparent feelings for him. As Claire watched, the adoration seemed to drain from the other woman's eyes. She looked as if she wanted to throw the pie at Dean.

"We don't talk much about his hernia, oddly enough." She turned to Claire. "Feel free to chat in here where it's warm. I'll be in the back for a while."

"Tell your parents hello for me, Gabby," Dean called after her.

"I'll do that," she said through gritted teeth, walking away, her chin and the pie held high.

Claire turned toward the handsome pharmacist. If he'd noticed Gabby's irritation, he didn't show it. He smiled.

"The reason I'm anxious to speak with you, Claire, is that a job has come up at the pharmacy."

Claire's heart began to pound. She told herself not to appear desperate. "Really. What kind of job?"

"Part-time, I'm afraid. I know you're looking for full." Either it was her imagination or Dean grew uncomfortable. "In fact, it probably wouldn't be more than a few hours each night. I'd want you to come in about a half hour before closing and then stay a couple of hours after, tidying and restocking the shelves. You'd be responsible for the soda fountain, too, cleaning the candy jars and wiping out the freezer. That kind of thing."

He named an hourly wage that seemed like too much for the tasks he required, but she wasn't about to look a gift horse in the mouth. Because the hours were short, the job wouldn't completely save her family from drowning, but it would keep them afloat awhile longer. Then, if she found an oven to use for her baking, they'd be better off than they'd been since moving to Oregon. That was something, anyway. It occurred to her she'd have to figure out childcare that wouldn't eat up her salary. Maybe a trade of some kind...

"I'll take the job," she said before she could worry herself out of it. Somehow, she'd make it work. "Just tell me when you want me to start."

Dean smiled at her instant acceptance. "Anytime. Whenever you can."

Telling him she'd phone him later that day, she shook on it with him, and Dean left. Excitement threaded through Claire's veins until she wanted to whoop like a halfback scoring a game-winning touchdown.

"Is he gone?" Gabby reentered with a broom and dustpan.

Claire nodded. "You're my good luck charm, Gabby. Dean Kingsley just gave me a job!"

"Great." The other woman tried to look enthusiastic. "At least one of us will get to see him more often."

"Oh, I'm sorry." Claire tilted her head sympathetically. "Have you felt this way a long time?"

Gabby shrugged. "Twenty-seven years or so. It'll pass."

"Twenty-seven years? And you've never told him?"

With sharp movements, Gabby began to sweep. "I tried to once, but Dean seemed determined not to understand what I was saying. I decided unrequited love would be easier than total humiliation. I may have miscalculated."

"Oh, my." Claire shook her head. "I guess I've never thought about how painful a crush could be."

"No more than appendicitis. Or pulling your fingernails off. Slowly." Collecting Claire's cut hair in the dustpan, she tipped it into the trash then looked up, miserable. "Have you ever had one?"

"What?"

"A bad crush."

"Me?" Claire blinked in surprise. "No. I was married."

Gabby snorted. "Before you were married. Did you and your husband have a crush on each other before you got together?" Hope put a small smile in her eyes.

"No." Claire began to feel vaguely uncomfortable. "I mean, I wouldn't say a 'crush' exactly." In an effort to convey that she'd always been too sensible to be infatuated, she chuckled. The sound emerged more uptight than wise. "I never wanted to have a crush. My mother was always falling in love with one man or another. The men tended to be drifters, but if the infatuation hadn't worn off by the time they were ready to move on, she'd pick us up and move after them. She'd follow them all over until they told her to stop or disappeared. I never wanted to be that out of control." Then she remembered what she'd been thinking prior to the haircut and blanched. She never had felt out of control around a man...until Fletcher kissed her.

Gabby looked at her with understanding. "I feel for your mother. An obsession is a hard thing to erase. Sometimes I'm afraid I might spend my entire life pining over Dean, even if he gets married to somebody else or I get married to somebody else. That's scary."

Shaking her newly shorn head, Claire stated adamantly, "That's exactly what I'm talking about. Love shouldn't make you feel that way. Love should make a person relax."

"You think so?" Gabby looked doubtful.

"Yes! Love—real love—is calming. It quiets your mind, so you can face reality and do the things you need to do in life without getting distracted and…overly emotional."

"So true love is like a tranquilizer?" Gabby's auburn brows arched. "I've definitely never looked at it that way before." Lapsing into a thoughtful silence, she finally shook her head. "No, Claire. I've lived calmly most of my life. I don't think it's all it's cracked up to be." Placing the dustpan on the floor, she resumed sweeping.

Claire watched her, a deeply uncomfortable feeling creeping through her limbs. Suddenly the image of Fletcher Kingsley filled her mind—the way he'd stared into her eyes after their kiss, his jaw tense, and his breath coming in hard puffs as if he'd run a long distance. With the memory of that look and of the kiss that had preceded it, Claire's lips began to tingle. Heat poured into her chest. Every cell in her body awakened as if an alarm clock had gone off.

Nearly all her life, she'd told herself she was happiest being average, feeling peaceful and steady. To reach sky-scraping heights you had to be willing to suffer bottom-of-the-barrel lows, and that was not for her.

*You're the youngest old woman I ever met, Claire Veronica.* Her mother's voice, sad and boozy, popped into her head. *At the rate you're going, you'll be in a wheelchair before you step foot on a dance floor. Me, I'm going to shake my booty all the way to the undertaker.* She'd done it, too. Didi had walked out of a Nashville nightclub in the wee hours one morning and crossed the path of a flat bed. Two witnesses said she'd been two-stepping across the street.

Claire bit her lip. It was true that she ran from frivolity the way some people ran from the IRS. She wasn't afraid of emotion—she loved her children to distraction—but living sanely and responsibly simply made life easier. And, yes, calmer.

Fletcher's kiss had rocketed her body way, way up. Nothing calming about that, but her disciplined mind had brought her back down to earth.

She certainly didn't intend to kiss him again and was equally certain he wouldn't try to kiss her.

Still, perhaps it was safe to admit—just this once and only to herself—that the feeling after Fletcher's kiss had been intoxicating. Addictive. She'd dipped into the well of memory several times since Saturday. All it took was the recollection of their lips together, their bodies inches apart, and once more she felt as if she were sitting at the top of a roller coaster, waiting breathlessly for a ride that would be dangerous and thrilling beyond belief.

Claire went to work for Dean the night after he offered her the job. Irene told her to look no further for a sitter, which enabled her to begin working at the pharmacy immediately. All the elderly neighbor asked in return was that Claire continue to bake for her bridge and bunko groups so she wouldn't have to buy "those hard-as-a-rock coffee cakes from that old goat Henry" at the bakery.

"You'll trade me a *babke* for a *bubbe*," she told Claire, using Yiddish words for coffee cake and grandmother.

Claire worked Tuesday through Friday that first week. Dean gave her a key so she could lock up after he and the other employees left, and each night she packed in as many tasks as she could before she went home. Even better, Gabby had offered to swap the use of her kitchen at home if Claire kept her supplied with molasses snaps, which meant Claire could fulfill her commitment to Irene and try to grow her home business.

Claire would have felt as if she'd won the lottery, save for two nagging concerns: she had no idea when she'd be able to buy a new stove for her own home, and it was obvious that Dean did not have enough work for her to do. He had a late-night crew that mopped the floors, cleaned the bathrooms and washed the windows, so on the fifth night of her new job, she decided to defrost and thoroughly wipe out the old freezer unit in the soda fountain.

She was elbow-deep in the freezer, scrubbing off a particularly gummy drip of coffee-chip ice cream when a knock sounded at the front. The other employees had long since gone home for the night, Dean was up in his apartment and the cleaning crew wasn't expected for another couple of hours yet, so Claire decided to continue with her task. The person rapping on the glass door proved more stubborn than she, however, so Claire sighed and headed for the front, intending to point to the closed sign and send the late arrival on his or her way.

The night was dark and moonless, but the light from the store clearly illuminated Fletcher on the other side of the glass. He appeared as surprised to see Claire as she was to see him.

Her nerves shot off like rockets. Fumbling with the keys Dean had given her, she awkwardly unlocked the door, and Fletcher entered, clad in a warm sheepskin-lined jacket and leather gloves. His ears were red from the cold.

"What are you doing here?" he said in lieu of "Hello."

"I work here. What are you doing here?" His heavy black hair had been cut since the last time she'd seen him, and she wondered if Gabby had had the honor.

"I need some ibuprofen."

"The pharmacy closes at six."

"I know that. I ate at the diner and decided to go for a walk. When I saw the lights on, I figured Dean was still working."

"No. He's upstairs." Claire's initial burst of nerves started to settle. "Didn't you already buy a bottle of ibuprofen on Friday?"

Fletcher's dark brows rose, if just a bit. His jaw worked a couple of times before he spoke. "Good memory."

She nodded. "Bad headache?"

"Stocking up."

Claire's gaze fell to his cane. When she returned to his face, she saw pride and a silent warning not to offer pity or compassion. So instead, she shrugged apologetically. "I can't run the cash register. Maybe you'd better come back tomorrow."

He nodded. "Why are you here at night?"

"I work at night."

"Every night?"

"Five evenings a week."

Fletcher's blue-gray eyes turned granite hard. "It's almost eight. How late do you work?"

His obvious irritation confused her. She peered at him. "Sorry, but are you asking for a specific reason? The last time we talked about a job, you made it crystal clear that was my concern and not yours."

He stared a moment then tipped his head. "Right." Glancing away as if he was searching for a word, he nodded to himself then looked back at her. "How's your oven?"

Anger swooshed up from Claire's belly. What was the matter with the man? He was an emotional yo-yo. Friday morning he'd told her never to darken his doorstep again. Friday afternoon he'd followed her home to fix her stove.

Saturday he'd told her he wanted her out of his house and out of his hair. Today he acted concerned about her. Every time she told herself to forget about him, he did something to make her feel cared for.

Putting her fists on her hips, Claire studied his face. "Is that honestly what you want to ask? 'How's your oven?'" When he appeared sincerely confused by the question, she flapped her arms against her side. "Fine. You need to stop talking to me now so I can get back to work."

"How are the boys?"

She glared at him. "Fine. They're just fine, thank you. Good night."

Turning, she stomped back to the soda fountain. When she looked over her shoulder, Fletcher had turned, too, and was heading for the door. Ignoring rational thought, she spun and stomped after him. Tugging on his sleeve when she caught up, she said, "I apologize. I don't even have a temper. I don't what it is about you."

His lips curved slightly.

"I mean, about me. When I'm around you. So, I'm sorry."

"You apologize too damn much."

"No, I don't. Only with you. I'm not offensive with other people." Realizing how offensive *that* sounded, she said, "Sorry."

He smiled wider.

"Damn it!" Then she clapped a hand over her mouth. "I never swear."

Fletcher laughed out loud. Slowly, she began to laugh with him. "I owe *you* the apology," he said.

She shrugged.

He sobered. "I'm sorry I kissed you. It won't happen again."

Claire no longer felt like laughing. "I know that. And if

you're apologizing for the kiss then I do owe you an apology, too."

"For what?"

"For kissing you back."

Her response kindled a smile in his eyes and curled the outer edge of his mouth. "You didn't kiss back."

"Yes, I—" As she realized what he was telling her, Claire snapped her mouth shut. She'd been married eight years. Before that, she'd practiced kissing on numerous pillows. Did Fletcher think her kissing was inept?

Humor changed the color of his eyes from winter gray to ocean blue, and Claire's cheeks grew hot. "When I say I kissed you," she prevaricated, "I mean I was trying to keep you from feeling awkward, not that I was *really* kissing you. If I'd been really kissing you...you'd have known it."

"Oh." Fletcher nodded. "Well, that was very kind. Sparing my feelings like that."

"You're welcome."

He cleared his throat. "So, if I were to kiss you again— which I'm not going to—but hypothetically, if I did..."

"I wouldn't kiss you back this time."

"You wouldn't."

She crossed her arms. "No."

"Okay." He crossed his arms, too. "Pity."

"Yeah." She nodded. "Why is it a pity?"

Fletcher leaned forward. "Because now I want to know how you kiss when you're *really* trying."

Claire couldn't swallow. Or blink.

Shrugging when she failed to move, he straightened. His lips curved in a sinuous smile, and Claire knew he was laughing at her. And suddenly it seemed imperative to wipe the smile off his face.

With more feeling than thought, she launched herself at

him, reaching up to pull his head toward hers, her hands on his cheeks as she pressed her lips to his.

The surprise of the attack must have kept him still at first. His gloved hands remained at his sides. A couple of seconds into the embrace, however, she felt his broad palm cupping the back of her head and his fingers delving into her newly clipped hair. One hand went to her lower back, and the cane he held tapped her lightly on the calves as he jerked her close. His mouth slanted across hers, his lips parted…and she stopped noticing anything at all after that.

The embrace turned into something raw and urgent, and she realized before long that even though she'd initiated it, he had taken charge.

The kiss began hard then turned soft. It started out warm then got hot. His teeth tugged her lips gently between his. He nibbled and tasted and then used his tongue.

So *this* was kissing. Intimate and all consuming, it made her dizzy. And if kissing him felt like this, then sex with Fletcher would be—

Claire felt faint. She wasn't sure exactly how the moment ended—*she* didn't end it—but at some point there was space again between their bodies, and he was holding her shoulders.

They stared at each other, their ragged breaths the only sound in the drugstore other than the hum of the freezer unit.

"You cut your hair." His raspy voice sounded as if he'd just woken up.

Claire couldn't speak at all.

"I like it." He stood there, looking as dazed as she felt, then let her go and took a step back. With a jerky nod, he left her, limping as quickly as he could to the front door. Without speaking to her again, he let himself out.

Claire followed slowly, locking up like a good employee and returning to her task at the soda fountain.

Even as her hands shook, she moved methodically, rhythmically scrubbing sticky ice cream from the freezer's interior. It was amazing that even in the midst of a mundane job, she could feel as if everything in the world had changed. *She* had changed. And as she worked, pretending to distract herself, she knew deep down that nothing would ever be the same for her again.

Fletcher sucked in cold air like a fish trying to breathe on land. He wanted the frigid night to wake him up, snap him out of the shock he was in.

He'd kissed an angel, and all he could think was *More. Give me more.*

He wanted to run his fingers through her sexy haircut, study her face and be with her while the sun rose outside the window. He wanted her to touch him.

Instead of returning to his truck and the solitude of the ranch, he walked straight around the block, through the alley and up the stairs to Dean's door. His brother answered after the first round of rapid-fire knocking.

"You were supposed to give her a real job." Without invitation, Fletcher strode past his brother, bringing his walking stick down hard as he propelled himself into the apartment. He step-thumped to the sofa, sat heavily and glared. "It's almost eight o'clock."

True to form, Dean calmly tilted his head as if the interruption to his evening caused only a mild curiosity. "And a 'real job' ends…when?"

"Don't be a wiseass." Pounding his cane like a hammer onto Dean's hardwood floor, Fletcher hauled himself up again and started to pace.

Dean sighed, closed the door and headed toward the kitchen. "Coffee?"

"No."

"Then maybe it's time you get to the point. It's been a long day. I'm looking forward to a quiet evening." Maintaining eye contact, he crossed his arms.

Realizing that his brother was unwilling to take any of the usual crap, Fletcher calmed down a bit. "All right." He removed a glove and rubbed his forehead, where a headache was beginning. "I came up here to tell you to give Claire a day job. So now that we've handled that, I'll be on my way."

Studying Fletcher carefully, Dean crossed to the coffee table. He picked up an empty mug and stared into it as if he were reading tea leaves. "What were you doing at the pharmacy after hours? Were you checking up on her?"

Fletcher's gaze whipped to his brother. "No. I ate at the diner and passed by here on my way home. When I saw the light, I figured you were still working, and I could get a bottle of ibuprofen."

"You just got a bottle of ibuprofen."

"And now I need another. So, how are you going to handle this?"

"I'm going to ask what kind of pain-management program your physician put you on."

"Not about the ibuprofen! About Claire."

Letting the coffee mug swing from his finger, he shrugged. "I already did what you asked me to do about Claire. I gave her a job."

"A night job." He gestured to the door leading to the pharmacy downstairs. "She can't put her kids to bed. Or read to them. Kids lose brain cells if they aren't read to at night." He narrowed his eyes. "You're in the medical field, you ought to know that."

"A night job is all I have, Fletcher." He shook his head.

"In truth, I don't even have that. I had to work Claire into the schedule in a way that wouldn't make my usual cleaning crew nervous. I don't want to scare anyone in this economy. I don't have enough jobs to go around."

"You've got to find her something else."

Dean craned his neck. "Are you hearing me? I made up this job. It's the best I can do."

"I told you I'd pay her salary."

"That's not the point. Also, it's crazy." Turning, he raised his voice as he walked to the kitchen. "Why don't you hire her? She needs a real job, and you must have more than enough to do at the ranch. Of course, I have no way of knowing that with any certainty as I haven't been invited out there since you've been back, but I imagine the place is a wreck. It was a rental for years."

Fletcher trailed his brother to the kitchen doorway, and Dean added, "You could work your land and give Claire some of the smaller jobs inside."

A grunt was all that suggestion merited. "You have no idea how asinine that is."

"Why?"

Because with Claire in his house, Fletcher wouldn't be able to get his mind out of the bedroom, that was why. "You said yourself the ranch is a mess. It's no place for a woman."

Dean was shaking his head before Fletcher finished the sentence. "Make sense at least." He began the process of preparing a fresh pot of coffee. "So what have you decided about the will?"

"What do you mean, what have I decided? I'm going to give the city a chance to sell me the property at a reasonable price, and if they don't take my offer, I'm going to sic a team of very aggressive lawyers on them."

"You haven't considered marriage at all?"

Instantly Fletcher thought of the moment when he'd kissed Claire.

"No," he lied flatly. "Now let's get back to—"

But Dean wasn't ready to let it go. "I know Dad and your mother had issues in their marriage, but—"

"Don't!" Anger, old but swift, rose with blinding intensity. "Do not trivialize what happened." Fletcher swore between clenched teeth. Feeling perspiration on his forehead, he backhanded it away. *Issues in their marriage.* Arguing over housework, disagreeing about where to send the kids to school—those were "issues." The disaster Victor Kingsley had made of his second marriage could not be compared.

Dean looked as if he wanted to say more, but wisely backed down.

Fletcher shook his head. By most accounts, Victor's marriage to Dean's mother had been less turbulent, though it, too, had ended in tragic loss when Lily died of cancer. Dean had been only five, the age Claire's younger son was now.

As far as Fletcher knew, Dean had never been engaged, or even close to it. Fletcher's own relationships typically ended after a few months, if they made it that far. A decent woman deserved better than a Kingsley male for a spouse. Their track records stank.

Fletcher's stomach began to feel sour. Even if he were willing to risk a bad marriage for himself, he didn't intend to watch someone else suffer for his shortcomings.

"Back to the topic at hand," he said, wanting to finish the conversation and get out of here. "What can you do for Claire?"

Taking time before he answered, Dean scooped ground coffee beans into a filter. "What's the story? You've known this woman for all of a week, and you're worried about her working at night?"

The confusion that was Fletcher's loyal companion of late

filled him with an uncomfortable, prickling heat. He felt claustrophobic in the small kitchen. He needed to get back into the cold air.

"I'm not worried. I was walking by and saw the light on.... I didn't expect her to be away from her kids, that's all. She's very protective of them."

With a sidelong glance and silence, Dean spoke all he needed to. Fletcher bristled. "You're the bleeding heart here," he accused his older brother. "You've got more donation canisters downstairs than things for sale. I expected you to give a single woman a job that would get her home before the *Late Show* comes on." He squinted. "Does she go to her car alone?" And then a new thought occurred. "Hell, she doesn't *walk home,* does she?"

"I didn't ask about her transportation plans."

With a mighty swear and crack of his cane against the door molding, Fletcher spun around so quickly, he lost balance and had to catch himself. Muttering about irresponsible employers, he step-thumped rapidly to the interior door of Dean's apartment—the one that led into the drugstore—and headed down the stairs, pretending he did not hear Dean's laughter following him into the pharmacy.

Claire was scraping the inside of the freezer when he made his way to the front of the store. The sight took him back about a dozen years to the time when he completed the same task, although he did it with far less concentration than she exhibited.

Fletcher slowed his steps and finally halted about a dozen feet away. Now that he was here, he didn't know what to say to her.

*Hi. I was afraid you'd be attacked on the streets of Honeyford on your way home.*

Or, *My brother's a shmuck for making you work nights.*

Or, the truth: *I can't stop thinking about you, and it's driving me crazy, and I'm not sure what to do about it.*

Breathing through the fact that he felt less sure of himself than he had in two decades, he wandered forward. A floor tile squeaked.

Claire froze. She was using a slab-style ice-cream scoop to scrape ice and gunk out of the ancient unit. Realizing she was no longer alone, she raised her head and turned toward the sound, wielding the stainless-steel utensil like a sword. As she held it in front of her, her eyes darted to locate the intruder, her face contorted into a mask of kick-ass fury. Unfortunately with her wispy hairdo, small features and interminably affable face, she looked more like Tinkerbell on uppers than Rambo. He wanted to hug her.

"It's me," he said, raising a steadying hand. "Fletcher." While she blinked, trying to work out how he'd gotten in, he moved slowly forward.

When they were close enough to touch, he took the ice cream scoop from her hands. Claire stared up at him. "What are you doing?"

"I'm an old pro at this," he told her, nodding to the freezer, but thinking of something else entirely. "Let me show you how it's done."

As he began to scrape with the steel scoop a smile bloomed in his chest and spread outward. Suddenly it didn't matter whether it was wrong or right, asinine or brilliant. He was going to hire Claire Dobbs to work for him.

## Chapter Ten

A day after Fletcher's appearance at the pharmacy, Claire stood in her new friend Gabby's quaint kitchen, baking and sharing conversation while Rosalind slept atop a quilt spread out on the living room floor, and the boys played in the yard with Gabby's Boston terrier, Humphrey. As Claire folded chocolate chips into the batter for sour-cream banana bread, Gabby's microwave beeped to announce that her low-fat, low-sodium, low-carb lunch was thoroughly heated.

"The box said chicken 'fiesta' burrito," Gabby muttered doubtfully, eyeing the contents of the tiny paper tray as she removed it from the oven. "Doesn't look like a party to me." She looked up at Claire, wrinkling her nose. "Do you have any spare sour cream?"

Claire smiled as she passed a pint container down the counter. "Won't that defeat the purpose?"

"Probably." Dipping a tablespoon into the container, Gabby pulled up a neat serving, making sure the sour cream in the spoon was completely level before she scraped it onto her burrito. Then she licked the spoon like a lollipop. "Nothing personal," she commented between licks, "but I'm kind of glad you're not going to be baking here anymore. Last night I dreamt my house was made of gingerbread, and I ate a hole in the roof. When I phoned the insurance company, they said bingeing was not covered by my policy, and I needed to be more disciplined." She shook her head sadly. "What's the world coming to when you can't eat what you want in your sleep?"

Laughing, Claire poured her batter into a loaf pan and tossed the mixing spoon in the sink. Since Fletcher had offered her a job, she'd given Dean two weeks' notice (which he'd graciously declined, increasing her suspicion that he'd given her the job out of kindness rather than necessity) and arranged with Fletcher to bake at his place during her workday. "You've been awfully sweet about letting me fill your kitchen with temptation," she told Gabby. "I can't tell you how much I've appreciated it."

"My pleasure." Dimples appeared in Gabby's peaches-and-cream cheeks. "The perks have been awesome." After a brief hesitation, she inquired, "So are you sure you feel good about working for Fletcher Kingsley?"

Though sincerely asked, the tone of the question made it seem almost ominous. "Yes. I feel good about it."

Perhaps "good" wasn't the most accurate description of Claire's feelings, and truthfully she would have liked to discuss the Kiss and all her tumultuous thoughts about Fletcher with someone. Unfortunately, like Mr. Garlock, Irene Gould and an apparent host of others, Gabby had a strong opinion about Fletcher that made her anything but neutral.

After helping her clean the soda fountain freezer, Fletcher had made Claire a job offer she couldn't refuse. The hours were perfect, the salary more than she'd ever made on a job and she could bring her children to work when school was out. As he described the situation, Fletcher had worked hard to convince her that, upon further reflection, he *needed* a cook-housekeeper. Although she agreed with him, she found his timing suspect. The job he offered would solve every problem that plagued her. He knew that.

"I realize there are people in town who aren't crazy about him—" she began.

"Understatement," Gabby interrupted, pulling a clean fork from the dishwasher and leaning against the counter to eat.

Turning away, Claire filled the sink with hot water so she could clean up from the afternoon's baking session. The rising steam perfectly reflected her rapidly changing mood. Why didn't people notice what she did about Fletcher? True, he was neither as suave nor as charming as Dean, but he had a conscience that never slept. His gruffness was a defense; she was sure of it. Something had hurt him badly in the past, and he was afraid to be hurt again.

Claire hadn't met one person she didn't like since coming to Honeyford. The townspeople were relaxed, humorous and, in an age when a lot folks kept to themselves, they seemed to go out of their way to help each other. Yet except for Sophie, who wanted to be plenty neighborly, no one bothered to make Fletcher feel welcomed home. He'd been away for ten years, yet people seemed keen to judge him based on the past.

Poking at her burrito, Gabby said, "It's hard to believe Fletcher and Dean had the same father, isn't it? They couldn't be more different. Of course, Fletcher's mother was a real nut. I don't remember her, but I've heard people say she was loonier than—"

"Stop!" Claire swung around. Surprise at Gabby's disclosure and at her own reaction to it made Claire's breath come fast and hard. It took a couple of seconds for the full impact of Gabby's words to hit, and then Claire was flat-out mad. "People gossip about his mother? That's terrible."

Gabby's light eyes widened. Her round cheeks turned pink. "I'm sorry. You're right—I don't know anything about his mother. But I do know something about Fletcher, and he's earned his bad reputation, Claire. I'm older than he is, and I remember what he was like in high school. He craved trouble, and he got into plenty of it. He had so many privileges and opportunities. His father owned half of Main Street back then. Everyone knew and respected Doc Kingsley. They'd have liked and respected Fletcher, too, if he'd tried to earn it at all. Even now, when he has the opportunity to change the entire town's opinion of him, he doesn't care enough to do it."

"What are you talking about?"

"I'm in the chamber of commerce, and I can tell you that almost every business in town is suffering. Someone got the idea to hold a big, weekend-long party in spring to try to pull in some of the tourists who typically go to Bend and Sisters but ignore Honeyford. So the idea was to start with a parade. We'd choose a Honey Queen to ride on a float, and there'd be a bake-off, a Bit O'Honey eating contest, things like that. But what would grab us the most attention from the big cities would be to have a celebrity as the grand marshal."

"And someone decided that celebrity should be Fletcher?" An uneasy feeling crept into Claire's stomach.

"Everyone decided it should be Fletcher. He's the only celebrity we've got." Halfheartedly, she cut a piece of the burrito with the edge of her fork. "The Chamber asked Dean if he would approach his brother on behalf of the town, but Dean declined. He said he thought it was a bad idea. We all know what that means—he's positive Fletcher won't even consider it."

Claire disagreed with Dean; she thought it was a very good

idea now that she'd heard the whole plan, and believed Dean should have presented the program to his brother. If Fletcher intended to make his home and his living in Honeyford then he would need a way to reclaim the goodwill of his neighbors. Someday he would have a family; the respect and support of the community would be important.

"Fletcher's not the ogre everyone assumes he is," she said with certainty. "If he understood what was at stake for the town, that businesses are suffering, he'd help out. I'm sure of it."

Gabby gazed at her quizzically. "How well do you know him? I thought you'd just met."

"We did, but…" It was a fact that Claire had been born practical. The trait had served her well through the years, but she didn't feel practical at all where Fletcher was concerned. "I don't know exactly what Fletcher did to anger people before, or why he did it," she said, "but I know he cares about people today. Why do you think he's giving me the perfect job?"

Gabby's eyes narrowed. "Because according to *US Magazine* he's dated half the female stars in Hollywood, and your new haircut makes you look like an actress? If I do say so myself." Raising her brows, she took another bite of the burrito.

Pleasure and disappointment chased each other around Claire's chest. The truth she'd been trying to ignore slapped her in the face: she'd been hoping the kiss meant something to him. Different from anything she'd experienced before— sexier, hungrier and more knowledgeable—that kiss would stay in her mind even if she knocked herself in the head with a mallet. It was as if she'd been a pot of cold water, and Fletcher's lips got her boiling before she'd even known the stove was on.

Reminding herself that she had no intention of becoming

romantically involved with a man, any man, she admitted nonetheless that she was developing feelings for Fletcher Kingsley. It was as foolish as it was true. He'd dated actresses; she was a widow with three children. A widow with more important concerns than to scratch an itch she hadn't had before she'd met him.

"He hired me because he knows I've got three kids and no job," she insisted, telling herself as well as Gabby. "He has a very strong conscience." Gabby's faintly skeptical frown spurred Claire to defend him further. "Fletcher would be glad to help out the town. It's not fair to judge him before anyone's even asked him to be grand marshal."

"We wanted him to emcee the Bit O'Honey eating contest, too." Gabby's expression turned speculative. "The Chamber of Commerce would be thrilled to have someone approach him. Do you want to?"

A tiny voice in Claire's head warned that she didn't know her subject nearly well enough to have insisted on anything, while another part of her wanted so badly to believe she was correct about Fletcher that "Yes" hovered on the tip of her tongue.

*The worst he can do is say no.*

But she had faith in him. A man who cared about widows and children would not ignore the well-being of an entire town. Fletcher was a good man; perhaps better than he realized. She was going to help him prove it.

"All right. Give me a couple of days to settle into the job, and then I'll ask." Her pulse accelerated, so she calmed herself with work, gathering the remaining baking utensils and slipping them into the hot, soapy water. She turned toward Gabby and saw that the skepticism was edging slowly toward admiration. Suddenly, unexpectedly, Claire felt that she was part of something, part of a family of souls that extended beyond her home. It was the feeling she'd been missing.

All the things she wanted to give her children—security, belonging, faith in the future—all that was waiting just around the corner. She was about to start a real job; she was making new friends. Fletcher Kingsley had already played a significant part in that story. She could return the favor by reuniting him with his hometown, one more thread woven into the tapestry of community.

She smiled, feeling at once lighter and more grounded than she had in ages. With a burst of confidence that felt like sunshine after a cloudy winter, she told Gabby, "This town is in for a surprise. I guarantee it."

Two hours into Claire's first day at the ranch, Fletcher knew he was certifiably a jackass.

With a bitter chill biting through his jacket and gloves, he used the pliers he'd found in his grandfather's toolbox to repair a sagging portion of wire fencing. The work felt like salvation. The November morning smelled like snow, and the throbbing in his leg and hip provided the beat by which he timed his days. He would have preferred to accomplish some indoor task today, but the moment Claire had arrived, he'd known he had to get as far from the house as possible.

When he'd hired her, he'd been full of lust and the notion that he was doing her a big fat favor by offering a steady income. Exploring the heat and fascination he felt for her seemed only a matter of time. There were, no doubt, names for bosses like him, but he didn't want to think about that. Especially as the moment he saw her today, lugging cleaning supplies and sacks of food, smiling like a kid happy with her supplies on the first day of school, he had known he couldn't touch her. Not while he was the boss and she the employee. He'd painted himself into a corner with only two routes of escape: fire her or ignore the attraction.

So here he was, ignoring...

And thinking about the ribbon of smoke that had begun curling from the chimney of his house about an hour ago...

And the song Claire had started to sing in a surprisingly earthy voice as soon as she'd set to work...

And the faded jeans that clung to her round bottom...

Tying the new and old wires together, he gave the pliers a hard twist. The old wire snapped.

"Damn!"

Fletcher sat on the hard ground and hung his head. The pliers clicked as he tossed them to the dirt.

As a boy, he'd felt such peace here on this ranch, toiling alongside his grandfather, who had owned and worked the land for decades. He had been able then to focus on a task. Satisfaction at the end of a challenging day had been a virtual guarantee.

Today, his thoughts zipped and pinged around the bumpers in his brain like crazed pinballs, never settling in one place, never yielding tranquility. It had been that way for years and years. Usually, he didn't even notice.

Sighing, he glanced over his shoulder, watching the translucent gray plume rise from his chimney like a smoke signal. *Come home...come home....*

Where the hell was home anymore? Before he'd arrived back in Honeyford, he had believed possessing this property, reestablishing it as a working ranch, making it the envy of the area was what he had to do before he could rest. But now Claire was in his house and, worse, in his mind, so there went all hope of peace.

Picking up the pliers, he ignored the physical discomfort as he pushed onto his good knee again and got back to work. He'd been distracted the past couple of weeks. He needed to attend to the will, call his lawyer, deal with the mess Victor had left. That would keep him plenty busy until his libido shut off again.

He stayed away from her until two thirty, when his growling stomach and the beginnings of a headache made him head for the house. Hoping the sliced turkey he'd bought a few days ago was still good, he planned to grab a quick sandwich, but the moment he opened the back door and peeked tentatively into the kitchen, savory aromas reached out to tug him all the way in.

Gravy dripped delicately down the sides of a large pot that bubbled on the stove. Stew. A round loaf of bread rested on the tile counter, and Fletcher could tell by the yeasty smell that it was freshly baked. He couldn't resist. Grabbing a bowl, he picked up the ladle Claire had been using and dished up his lunch.

He ate in the kitchen, leaning against the counter, knowing the stew was the best meal he'd had in... Hell, maybe ever.

When he was done, he washed and dried the bowl, cleaned up the bread crumbs and told himself to beat it before she found him there. But he convinced himself that he needed a warmer sweater and started down the hall toward his bedroom. He glanced left and right into various rooms as he went, looking, despite himself, for the woman who so naturally left home and comfort in her wake. He found her, finally, at the back of the house, in his bedroom, staring at the bookshelf he'd set up in there, a duster under her arm and a leather-bound novel in her hands.

She was shoeless, a pair of thick purple socks warming her small feet. Her deep amethyst sweater ended just above the beltline of her jeans, revealing a thin slice of milky white skin. Under her cap of short hair, she frowned as she perused the book.

He wanted to speak, to say something light or relating to the meal she'd made, but his throat went dry. Without actually meaning to, he stepped into the room, and the floor beneath the carpet squeaked.

When their eyes met, Claire smiled. "You have a lot of books."

He nodded. And took several steps farther into the room. "You sound surprised."

She lowered the book and turned toward him. "I left some lunch for you—"

"I had it. The stew was excellent." Plucking the book from her hands, he looked at the cover. "*The House of Seven Gables.* You like Nathaniel Hawthorne?"

Her eyes lowered to the cover of the book then flicked back to him. "Do you?"

Gently, he pulled the volume from her grasp. Hardly recognizing his own actions, he opened the book to a page he'd dog-eared a long time ago and read aloud. "'What other dungeon is so dark as one's own heart! What jailer so inexorable as one's self!'" Then he looked again at Claire, feeling ridiculous.

Her frown deepened. "Do you believe that?" she responded after a time. "That the heart is a dungeon?"

"It can be."

She looked at the crammed shelves. "Have you read all those books?"

"Most. I was such a screw-off in high school, I figured I had a lot of catching up to do." He turned the Hawthorne novel over in his hands. The fact that he read voraciously had always felt like a private matter; hence, the presence of a bookcase in his bedroom rather than the den or living room. After years of presenting himself as someone who just didn't give a damn, the polar opposite of his brother and father, he'd have felt foolish having people see a library of classic novels that were dog-eared and written in. And yet, he felt a strange relief having Claire stand here in front of his "secret."

"Why do your kids have Shakespearean names?" he

probed, wanting to own a piece of information about her, too.

Her eyes flickered with a sweet bashfulness. "Coincidence?"

A smile rose to his lips, and he wondered how long he could keep her here, talking. "Try again."

Glancing away, she plucked *The House of Seven Gables* from his hands and carried it back to the bookcase, stroking one hand over the cover as if it had creases she needed to smooth. Carefully returning the novel to the shelf, she settled it neatly among the others. For the first time, Fletcher noticed that she had tidied the shelves, aligning the books' spines.

"I love to read," she murmured, studying his library, and he wished she'd turn around. "When I was seven, the school I was in had a gift drive for the families in need. I got a book. *Frog and Toad Together.* It was hardcover, and I loved it. I don't know if I'd ever owned a book before. I may have, but we moved so much that things probably got lost in the shuffle." She ran the duster lightly along the shelves he was sure she'd already cleaned.

Fletcher inched closer. Moving didn't account for why she had no memory of owning a book. If he thought about it, he could still recall counting sleepers with Dr. Seuss and hoping the duck would escape a spanking every time his mother read him *The Story About Ping.* When you were read to, you remembered. It was as simple as that. He leaned forward to hear her next, quiet words.

"I slept with *Frog and Toad* in my arms every night. And I never let the book out of my sight for more than a few hours during the day, because I was sure my mother would box everything if we moved and forget to pack it."

Her laugh wobbled. Though the sound lacked self-pity, Fletcher found no humor in the story she was telling. The conversation was beginning to feel like a paint-by-numbers picture, each tiny colored-in block contributing to a fuller picture of Claire Dobbs and her ferocious commitment to motherhood.

"Do you still have the book?" he asked.

She did look at him then, and nodded. "I read it all the way through for the first time when I was fourteen."

She waited, her large hazel eyes patient and unwavering as he worked out the implication. "You couldn't read it before then."

She shook her head slowly. "I used to think I was slow, because I didn't keep up with the kids in my grade. I was so ashamed. I cut classes every time we moved so no one would know how behind I was. By the time we landed in Kentucky, I was fourteen, but belonged in elementary school."

Anger flared like brush fire inside Fletcher. He struggled to keep his expression neutral so she would continue talking, but he was furious with her parents, the schools that had let her slip through the cracks and the kids who had intimidated her to the point that she'd cut class. The dormant teen inside him wanted to tell her to screw them all. Who needed school?

At twenty-eight, however, he knew that man could not live by rebellion alone. Knowledge was power in more ways than he'd realized at seventeen. And Claire deserved power.

"What happened when you were fourteen?" he asked, wishing they could sit down, talk the way two average people getting to know each other might have. But they were in his bedroom, and the only place to sit was intended for sleeping or sex. He stood where he was and waited for her answer.

"I went to school that first day in Kentucky. I didn't think I'd stay, but when the teacher realized I couldn't read, she didn't talk about special needs. She asked me questions about where I'd gone to school and how I liked to learn and what my goals were. I couldn't answer anything except the part about previous schools." Claire offered a brief shrug. "Mrs. Karp started tutoring me after school, then on the weekends, too. We'd study in her kitchen, and afterwards she'd cook and bake while I read the recipes aloud to her. I loved it. For the first time in my life I had…" She paused, the heartache and hope of her past glittering in her eyes. "I had respect. From her and for myself." The emotion in her expression faded slowly, replaced by a pragmatism he could only admire. "I knew then that a good education would be one of the best gifts I could give my children, and as long as I'm breathing, that's exactly what they're going to get."

In that moment, Fletcher realized that, despite her marriage, she'd had plenty of practice waging solo wars. His fingers twitched with the urge to touch her. "I skipped my high school graduation. Didn't like the cap and gown look," he said, trying to gain distance by lightening the moment. "I bet you looked cute in yours."

She smiled. "I hadn't caught up enough to graduate with my class. Mrs. Karp wanted me to keep working at it, and I guess I should have, but I'd met Arlo by then."

"So you got your GED?"

"No. Didi, my mother, was set on moving to Tennessee, but I didn't want to move again, so Arlo and I got married, and I went to work. I don't have a diploma or my GED." She shook her head quickly, making her bangs fall into her eyes. "That won't happen with my kids. They're going to graduate high school. And then go to college."

"And the Shakespearean names?" he asked.

"Good omens."

A beautiful stubbornness and frightening faith filled her face. She wanted it so badly, the opportunity for her children that she'd never had for herself. Fletcher wanted to warn her not to be certain of anything. People couldn't be expected to move like trains, along tracks that had been laid down years before. He ought to know. But expectations were addictive; even when resentment seemed to be their natural outcome, they were difficult to give up.

He couldn't begin to understand her, this woman for whom commitment and sacrifice for others were a way of life. But the desire to shield her from disappointment rose strongly inside him, and he figured that might be as close as he was going to get to magnanimous.

"Who looks out for you?" he asked, his voice quiet and hoarse, as if he'd smoked too many cigarettes in his life.

She looked surprised by the question, one she clearly had not asked herself.

Lightening struck Fletcher then, an electric shock that rearranged a lifetime of isolation. His noble intentions to leave her alone burned up and blew away.

Closing the last bit of distance between them, he raised an arm and his fingertips brushed her cheek; it was so soft a snowflake would have slid right off.

Fletcher moved slowly, giving her time to stop him. And praying that she wouldn't. In his entire life, he couldn't remember a moment when he'd wanted so badly to give rather than take.

She stood still, the feather duster in the crook of her arm, her hands motionless. He took that as a green light.

Brushing thick, short locks of blond hair gently behind her left ear, he let his fingers slide inside the collar of her purple sweater. Her neck felt thin and delicate as he curved his hand around the nape, his eyes locked with hers all the while, asking if this was okay, telling her to trust him. For the longest while, his hands told her what his voice could not.

*I've never met anyone like you.*

Most of the time, the world felt dirty, overused, like a city sidewalk. In this moment, with Claire, the air was sweet, the grass green....

*You make me forget. Stay with me...let me hold you....*

He thumbed away the worry between her brows, delved his fingers into her hair and spread one hand across her back as he drew her closer without resistance....

*I want to give you what you give me...rest...comfort...if only in this place....*

Fletcher lowered his mouth to Claire's—slowly, testing— and their warm breaths mingled. He kissed the space above her upper lip. The corner of her mouth. He touched his forehead to hers and stayed there awhile, stroking her temple, her cheek and then, far more gently than he ever had with a woman, he took her mouth in a kiss that continued the conversation his hands had begun.

And then she was kissing him, too. Her hands moved around his back. Small and untutored and strong, they pressed and clung, rubbed and clutched. He wanted to laugh at the irony of it all. He, a man who'd been having sex since he was sixteen, had never felt so crazy, so hungry, so lustful or yearning, even though he'd been with women who'd have had his clothes and theirs off by now, and who would be capable of showing *him* a thing or two.

He could tell from Claire's kisses that he would be the tutor in their sexual relationship, and that was fine by him. She'd been married, but her husband had left a lot for another man to teach. Knowing he was going to be that man turned Fletcher's mind on and his body hard as a rock. He moved his pelvis slightly away, so he wouldn't frighten her. Then she moaned into his mouth, a tiny needful sound, and the threads of his control snapped. The hand he'd splayed on her back moved down to grasp her buttocks. He bent his knees and lifted her slightly at the same time, leaving her with no doubt about his current state or his intentions.

"I want you. All of you." The words were a low growl

against her sweet lips. "Tell me if it's too soon. But tell me now."

It seemed to Fletcher that an eternity passed while he held her closer than, perhaps, he should have. He realized later the only thing postponing her response was the difficulty she had moving inside his embrace. Once she'd wriggled slightly free, she wound her arms around his neck, pressing her ripe breasts against his chest as if she wanted to melt into him. She opened her mouth and let her tongue dance with his. That solid, aching part of him that wanted to burst through his jeans, and which he'd thought might scare her, didn't seem to frighten her in the least….

He laid her on the bed, beneath him, as quickly as he could. Making a mental note to tell her never to wear jeans to work again, he fumbled with the snap and zipper until he was able to strip them off her body with her still clinging to his neck.

When she was naked from the waist down, he reached for his fly and then stopped. That was the way he would have done it with another woman. Not with Claire. He took a breath, slowed himself down and felt his heart clench as he looked at her.

Petite and round, her body was as real and earthy as the woman inside. As he lifted away from her, she looked at him with eyes that were wide as lakes and reached for the hem of her sweater. Peeling it over her head, she dropped it gently to the floor and reached around to unclasp her bra. It was plain beige cotton, only a shade or two lighter than her skin, and it didn't completely embrace the swell of her breasts. At the moment, Fletcher thought it was the most beautiful undergarment he'd ever seen, but she deserved better, and he made another mental note—to buy Claire lingerie that was worthy of her.

Before the bra was unclasped, he moved forward and

brushed her hands away. Keeping his eyes on hers, he finished the job, freeing her body for his look and his touch. With the material gone, his gaze lowered. Slowly and as carefully as he could at first, he let his hands then his lips, tongue and finally his teeth follow the direction of his eyes.

Claire slid lower on the bed she had earlier made, moaning and running her hands through Fletcher's hair. He reached down and found her, not sure whose body reacted more strongly to his first exploratory invasion—his or hers. In a move that took him completely by surprise, she fisted her fingers in his hair and tugged him away from her. When his surprised eyes met hers, she panted as adamantly as anyone could, "Get undressed."

Fletcher grinned. Sitting up, he started unbuttoning as quickly as he could, but she wasn't content to watch. Her small hands tangled with his as they got rid of his clothes, her eager help stretching his ability to behave himself to the breaking point. Grappling for his wallet and the lone condom he'd stored there only a few days earlier, he sheathed himself quickly, not looking at her this time. When he glanced up again, Claire was reaching for him, and that simple gesture broke him loose.

He had her underneath him again in no time. His hands gripped her hips; his knees edged hers wide apart—he needed her to know he meant business. He'd never felt like this and figured he finally understood how a bull felt coming out of the shoot. He was as close to losing control with a woman as he'd ever been.

Holding her absolutely still, he stared at her hard and grunted, "This is it. Last chance. Then you're mine and nothing's going to stop me."

Claire's face was flushed, her breath labored. "So far,

you're the only one in this room who's used the word, 'stop.'" A sexy smile curved her lips.

Fletcher lowered himself the rest of the way, and for the next hour, they didn't stop at all.

## Chapter Eleven

"And then me and Ian—"

"Ian and I."

"Okay. Me and Ian and I ranned all around his yard and swang from a rope swing tied to a tree, and his mom said to stay outside until we was worned out, 'cept we never did get worned out, so we went back in for cookies…"

Orlando rattled on, more awake than Claire wished at eight o'clock on a weeknight, but his after-school playdate had been exciting beyond words, and he'd described it in detail repeatedly since Claire had picked him and his brother up at the Rolofsons' house.

The playdate had been arranged last week, so Claire wouldn't have to rush home on the first day of her new job, but she hadn't intended to spend that extra time in bed with her employer. Thankfully, she'd been too busy since leaving Fletcher to overthink anything.

She glanced at Will, who lay quietly beside his younger

brother, one arm crooked behind his head in a manly fashion. "How about you? You haven't said much about today. Did you have fun with Zeke?"

"Ian and Zeke's mom divorced their dad," he said in lieu of answering. "She says raising two boys by herself can sure suck the life out of a girl."

Claire's mouth opened so far, she heard her jaw click. "You heard Gina say that? Did she say it in front of Ian and Zeke?"

Will shook his head. "She was on the phone. But I wasn't eavesdropping. I was getting a drink of water." His eyes adopted the too-sober look that Claire wished with all her heart she could erase. "You may need to get married again, Mom."

Controlling herself, Claire glanced at Orlando, who seemed blissfully unconcerned by the turn their bedtime talk had taken, his concentration consumed by a secondhand Buzz Lightyear doll he was zooming through the air over his head. Focusing on William, Claire scooted higher on the bed. His hands lay folded atop the blanket. She covered them with her own.

"My children *give* me life, Will. That's probably the best thing about becoming a parent. You give your babies life, and then they return the favor, in so many ways. Why, sometimes after a hard day, all I have to do is look at you or Orlando or Rozzy, and I feel like my heart is a ball of sunshine. I feel that big and warm and happy."

Will squeezed her hand. She squeezed back, hoping she'd set his mind to rest, but he wasn't through yet.

"You didn't have to work so much before Dad died. There's three of us and only one of you. We need another adult around here, so it'll be fair."

"Will—"

"I'm almost an adult, Mom. I am," he emphasized before she had a chance to demur. "I'm going to be eight in July."

He looked so determined and so hopeful that Claire longed to answer well. Grateful Orlando was still absorbed in his own play so he wouldn't scoff at his brother, she told her eldest, "Thank you so much, buddy. You are one of my heroes, and I appreciate any help you give me." Lifting his hands, she gave them a quick kiss. "The thing is, part of a parent's job is to let their kids have fun, so even though we're a team, and I need your help *sometimes,* it would break my heart if all you did was work—"

"You work."

"Yes, but—" She almost told him that she'd had her turn to play, but the words wouldn't form. In her childhood, play had always come after other concerns, like feeling safe. As an adult, play took a backseat to responsibilities. Looking at her son's serious face, she changed tracks. "Tell you what. I'll start playing more if you agree to worry less." She brought her face close to his, touching noses. "What do you say? 'Cause we're okay, buddy. We're doing really, really well now."

A smile turned Will's little-boy lips up at the corners. "Okay, Mom. But I am getting older."

"I know you are."

She kissed him and Orlando and Buzz Lightyear, clicked on a nightlight and closed the door as she exited the room. For a while, she remained outside the boys' room, feeling as if she ought to stand guard. There were times when she wanted so badly to protect her children from pain that she had to stop herself from following them around.

Now she wondered if, despite all her efforts, history was repeating itself. Would Will grow up as she had, adult concerns overshadowing his childhood?

Downstairs, she paused in front of the photos on her fireplace mantel. There was one of Arlo and the boys holding fishing poles, excited and grinning as they set off on an adventure the summer before Arlo died. Claire was behind the camera. She'd remained at home that day, just a few months pregnant with Rosalind, taking in ironing for extra cash rather than enjoying the summer day with her family. Arlo had been working; they'd had health insurance. Claire could have enjoyed the day with her family, but that hadn't been her way. It still wasn't. And maybe that was the problem. Perhaps the best way to protect her children would be to *show* them how to live. When was the last time she'd taken a few hours off from work and from worry simply to play?

*This afternoon.*

Standing before the photo of her late husband, Claire blushed. Moving away, she straightened the sofa and gathered Rosalind's toys as she recalled the myriad surprises of this afternoon.

Fletcher—he was the first surprise. She'd already figured out that his bluster and his man-as-an-island routine were cover-ups. What she hadn't expected were the care, gentleness and dedication to her pleasure before he considered his own. And the biggest, most unexpected revelation of the day was the way she felt in his arms.

Excited, important, carefree... For the first time in her life, Claire knew what it was like to lose herself and to find herself in exactly the same moment.

Never in her life had she expected to make love with a man who wasn't her husband and who occupied no clear place in her life. She'd had sex, pure and simple.

With Arlo, she'd known she was moving away from the life her mother had led, away from the endless search for excitement and pleasure. Arlo had been her future, not simply a moment in time.

Fletcher's kiss had made her so mindless, she hadn't cared whether they spent one hour or one year together. This afternoon, all she'd known for sure was that denying herself the time in his arms—and in his bed—would have been like denying herself air to breathe.

They hadn't said they would have sex again, hadn't whispered promises or bogus words of affection. They had dressed quietly after the fact, each immersed in private thoughts. Claire couldn't guess at his, but hers had been conflicted: she'd slept with her employer on her first day of work. For a woman who hadn't made love to anyone other than the man she'd married, that kind of behavior should have felt appalling. Yet she'd been unable to stir up any instant regret.

She'd spent a lifetime trying not to be her mother, denying herself pleasure as if its pursuit could bring down a country or blow up a continent. Now she knew that she was a wife, a widow, a mother—a good mother—and that she wasn't going anywhere, wouldn't turn her life inside out in pursuit of a man. But the sex had been wonderful, thrilling, satisfying, and she wondered if she would do it again.

Would Fletcher expect it? She had sort of set a precedent.

There was no time to answer that question. Her doorbell rang. The clock on the mantel read eight forty-three. She knew who it was before she opened the door, and her heart galloped at the first sight of Fletcher, the perfect cowboy in his leather jacket, his black hair windswept. As always, his intense gaze focused on her with laserlike precision.

Under the circumstances, what was she supposed to do? Launch herself into his arms the way a lover might, or ask her boss what he needed this late at night?

"I brought you some things," he said before she had to decide. "May I come in?"

Claire stepped back from the door, reminded immediately of what she'd briefly forgotten: she trusted him. He didn't smile as he walked by, but his behavior seemed no different from what it had been prior to this afternoon.

Walking to the coffee table, Fletcher deposited a brown-paper grocery bag on its surface. "So. Your kids have Shakespearean names. Does that mean you've actually read Shakespeare?"

"I own a *Complete Works*."

"Good." He nodded. "This shouldn't be hard then."

Claire wasn't ready for a big discussion about this afternoon, but avoiding the topic completely in favor of Shakespeare was carrying "casual" a bit too far. Frowning, she asked, "What shouldn't be hard?"

"Helping you get your GED." The paper bag crackled as he unrolled the top and reached inside. "There are a lot of study guides out there." He revealed a large, thick paperback. "This one seems like a good start. It has a pretest and basic information. Once we know your strengths and weaknesses, we'll purchase guides on individual subjects, although I already bought the science guide to look over, because that's my weakest area." Dipping into the bag again, he came up with several dog-eared paperbacks she recognized from his bookshelf. "I figure we may as well dive into classic literature, too." Seating himself on her sofa, he spread the books, study guides, a spiral notebook and sharpened pencils on the table.

Claire felt disoriented. "I'm not getting my GED."

He looked up. "Yes, you are." His oceanic eyes, the ones that had stormed at her only a few hours earlier, now filled with purpose and understanding. "You're bright. And capable. You deserve a GED. And you should have it to compete in the job market."

"Are you firing me?"

His lips parted in a slow, sexy grin that showed movie star-worthy white teeth. "Hell, no." The smolder returned to his eyes. "I'm not nearly ready for you to spend your days anywhere else."

Claire relaxed before she even realized she was tense. Attraction sizzled along the line of their gazes. When Fletcher looked at her like that, she knew without doubt she wasn't ready to end the more intimate part of their relationship.

Crossing to the sofa, she stood in front of him, staring down, studying his hair, his face, remembering the feeling of being wrapped in his big arms. She reached for one of the books. "Huckleberry Finn."

"A classic." His voice cracked, which made her smile.

"I've read it." Holding it close to her chest, she looked at him sulkily. "Do I get extra credit?" He looked as if his mouth had gone dry. Feeling her power, Claire set the book on the table and picked up a different one. "Viktor Frankl, *Man's Search for Meaning.* I read that one with Mrs. Karp." She shook her head sadly. "I don't think you brought enough for me to work on tonight. Of course, I could take the pretest. But you know which subject I *really* need extra tutoring in?"

His Adam's apple moved visibly as he swallowed. "Which?"

"Phys ed. I used to cut that class all the time. I feel way behind."

"That's bad." Fletcher stood. Their bodies were so close she'd have to back up if she wanted to move. "I appreciate your telling me how I can help. Keep doing that." He pulled the Frankl volume from her hands and dropped it onto the table. She expected him to touch her, but he kept his hands by his sides. "The thing about P.E.…you need a dedicated gym." He glanced toward the stairs. "So you don't wake anyone up. I figured we could work on your GED at night."

Claire smiled. She remembered from talking to her girl-friends in Kentucky that some men felt skittish about making love with a child in the house. Those men had to be reminded how kids got siblings.

She took a tiny step forward, which pretty much plastered

her body up against his, but she was very, very good and kept her hands to herself. "My children sleep like stones," she said, looking up at his handsome, desire-filled face. "And this sofa here? It's a sleeper. Now—" her voice dropped to a near-whisper "—I'm willing to hit the books first thing, but I hear that physical activity improves the mind."

The pleasure that filled Fletcher's face was a beautiful sight to behold. His big, strong arms felt every bit as safe as they had that afternoon, and he held her with the same tenderness and desire that had made her limp before. Claire pressed her hands to his back, exploring the muscles, clutching him as tightly as she dared, reminding herself all the while that this wasn't forever.

He leaned down to kiss her, and as their mouths met, she remembered that *for now* was all they needed.

For the next week, Fletcher worked and made love with Claire during the day. In the evenings, he went to her house to help her study for the GED. The first few times he deliberately arrived after her children's bedtime, telling himself it would be easier for her if she wasn't forced to split her focus. The truth was less noble: the older boy, Will, made Fletcher nervous, with his too-solemn, too-perceptive stare.

One evening, however, despite his best attempts, Fletcher arrived while action still rang throughout the house. Friday night was movie night, apparently, at Claire's.

"You're just in time to help us decide," she said as she swung open the front door.

He tried to leave when he saw the boys galloping through the living room, Orlando on a hobbyhorse and Will astride what appeared to be a sawed-off broomstick, but Claire wouldn't hear of it. Will stopped and stared, as usual, then came to stand beside his mother, the broom handle planted in the carpet like a pitchfork.

"Decide what?" Fletcher asked, wondering how the gaze of someone he outweighed by a good hundred and thirty pounds could intimidate him.

"Should we have popcorn or chocolate chip cookies while we watch *Dreamer?* Will's vote is popcorn, but Orlando doesn't think he'll live to see another day without a cookie."

Dressed in a long-sleeved T-shirt and sweatpants that only hinted at the curves he was coming to know very well, Claire looked relaxed, happy and cuter than any of the rodeo groupies who wore jeans so tight it made a man wonder whether they'd managed to fit a thong under the denim.

Claire took his hand, forcibly drawing Fletcher into the fray, and he noticed that her small, perfect feet were covered in fuzzy blue slippers. Just the sight of her made him smile. Every day.

"What do you say?" She grinned. "You're the guest, so we'll let you cast the deciding vote. Popcorn or chocolate chip cookies?"

Immediately, Orlando began to chant, "Cook-ies! Cookies!" as he loped around on his stick-horse. Will, on the other hand, frowned at the sight of his mother's hand on Fletcher's arm.

Fletcher thought a beer might make watching a movie with a kid who hated him more palatable. Rather than voicing that thought, he sized up his competition and responded, "Both. You need popcorn *and* something chocolate to make it a real movie night."

Claire glanced at Orlando, and they shared exaggerated nods. She returned her gaze to Fletcher. "Okay. You're in charge of the popcorn. Come on, Orlie." She headed for the kitchen, waving her younger son along with her. "I need my cookie assistant."

She left Fletcher and Will standing in the living room, staring at each other.

"We make *our* popcorn in a pot," Will said, his voice rife with challenge and the derision only a seven-year-old could utter so remorselessly, "*not* in the microwave."

Clearly implying that Fletcher, clod that he was, used the inferior method.

"My grandfather made popcorn in a pot when I was your age."

Will's pale brows raised one tiny increment. "You're a lot older now, though. You'll probably burn it unless I show you how."

"Yeah. Probably."

The boy turned, headless stick in hand, to follow his mother's path to the kitchen. Fletcher followed. The pain in his leg and hip had diminished considerably after the massage Claire had insisted on giving him (he'd rewarded her thoroughly afterwards). Even though he hadn't used his cane in several days, Fletcher thought his gait was smoother.

"So what happened to the head on your hobbyhorse?" he asked Will as they entered the dining room.

"What do you mean?"

Fletcher pointed to the plain stick in the boy's hand. Will looked from it to Fletcher, his pale cheeks growing red. "It's not a hobbyhorse. It's a broken broom."

"Do you and your brother take turns with the hobby-horse?"

"No! It's for little kids. I only play horses because Orlando still likes to." Leaving the broomstick against the wall in the dining room, he marched away.

His belligerence told Fletcher more than words could have. Dropping the subject for the time being, Fletcher followed Will into the kitchen to make the popcorn.

While Claire and Orlando happily mixed cookie dough,

Fletcher allowed Will to order him around. He caught Claire's frown when Will loudly complained that Fletcher poured too much oil in the pot, but he gave his lover and the mother of this boy-man a brief shake of his head.

When they were ready to pour the popcorn into a bowl, Fletcher told Will, "It didn't burn. You're a good teacher."

Will didn't exactly *smile,* but he did look at Fletcher with less overt hostility.

"You taught me how to make popcorn the *right* way. How about if I teach you something? Something I know quite a bit about. Tomorrow?"

Will shrugged, but Fletcher saw a flicker of curiosity cross his face.

"Have your mother bring you to the ranch at ten o'clock, if she's free." He spoke loudly enough for Claire to hear. She nodded, smiling.

"Can Orlando come, too?" Will asked.

"Yep." Fletcher lowered his voice. "I respect you for asking. Looking out for your brother is a good thing." The moment the words were out, Fletcher realized that once again, someone in this small family had pulled him up short.

Family. He'd avoided it for years. Now it was all around him.

Saturday began as the kind of central Oregon day that ensured smoke would be spiraling up from every chimney, scenting the air with fir and ash. Indoors, coffee dripped and thermoses of hot cocoa and cider were filled, promising something sweet and warm when the cold bit through the thickest of garments.

Fletcher had been working in the barn for four hours by the time Claire pulled up with her children in tow. Orlando slipped from the car, eager to explore every stall. Will was curious but moved more slowly, and Claire approached with Rosalind in her arms. She met Fletcher at the barn door.

"You were wonderful with Will," she said first thing, repeating the sentiment she'd whispered in his ear as he'd left last night. "It took forever to get the boys to bed. They were so excited about their surprise today."

Fletcher ached to take Claire in his arms. He felt so damn different when she was around. As if everything that had come before was a tidal wave, and she was the sun and balmy air after the storm. Because the boys were behind them, exploring the barn, he kept his hands to himself.

"Are you going to stick around today?" he asked, letting his eyes tell her how much he'd like to close the space between them.

"That was the plan. What's the big surprise we're waiting for?"

"Patience," he said, anticipating her reaction to the day as much as he was anticipating Will's and Orlando's.

They didn't have long to wait. Tires crunched along the gravel driveway, signaling the arrival of two pickup trucks, each hauling a horse trailer.

"Will! Orlando!" Fletcher called over his shoulder. "Front and center. The horses are here."

"Horses? Real ones?" Orlando's joyful cry brought a smile to Fletcher's face. Small feet stampeded through the barn until the boys stood before him, gawking at the vehicles that crunched slowly up the driveway.

"Are there really horses in there?" Will asked in his quiet way.

"There are," Fletcher answered. "And more coming in a few days. We'll get this group settled first."

"Can we touch them?"

As much as he was able, given his own pleasure in the moment, Fletcher affected a frown. "Can you? You *have* to.

I'm expecting you two men to do a fair share of the work." He nodded toward the approaching trailers. "Today we'll be unloading three quarter horses and a pony named Misty. You're responsible for introducing Misty to her new stall. Later today I'll show you how to groom her."

The boys looked at each other, openmouthed, then nodded eagerly at Fletcher. "I know how to ride ponies!" Orlando exclaimed, vibrating with delight. "I can ride wild broncs, too. I'm good at it! Are we gonna ride her? Are we?"

Aware that neither boy had ridden anything more than a hobby horse, Fletcher struggled to keep a straight face. "First you'll learn how to care for the mare. Then we'll talk about riding. Right now, it would be a good idea to run to the house and ask your mom to cut up some carrots. Big chunks, but not too many. After Misty's relaxed a bit, we'll give her a snack."

Watching the boys race each other to the house, Fletcher felt a pinch of emotion—as if he needed to take a deep breath, but couldn't.

Receiving the horses he'd bought a couple of weeks ago was understandably a source of satisfaction. Though he'd planned for more than a decade to turn his grandfather's ranch into the finest spread in Oregon, that did not account for the swell of feeling in his chest. Winning rodeo championships had satisfied him, too. Earning more money in a year than most folks in Honeyford earned in a lifetime had satisfied him. This was something more.

A sudden stinging behind his eyes brought him up short. *What the devil?*

The excitement of Claire's sons, innocent and infectious, made him feel…happy. A pure kind of happy he had known a long time ago. And now, for the first time in memory, he felt proud, not only of what he had accomplished, but of himself.

Buying the pony for Claire's sons had felt like a whim at the time. Now he knew it was the finest inspiration he'd had in years.

Claire spent the late morning and early afternoon playing with Rosalind while Fletcher taught the boys everything they'd ever wanted to know about horses. In all, seven animals moved into Pine Road Ranch that day, with Will and Orlando helping throughout the process.

Fletcher explained that the stock was comprised of American Quarter Horses, though one of the animals was quite a bit smaller and a good deal older than the others. Its name was Misty River, and after the boys joined Claire in the house for lunch, Misty was saddled and waiting for them to take a ride around the corral.

As soon as she'd settled Rosalind down for a nap on Fletcher's bed, she hurried to the front of the house so she could watch her boys from the kitchen door. *Her boys.* When she thought those words, she included Fletcher. And, indeed, there he was, holding Misty's bridle and nodding to Will as he led them around the corral. Orlando was stationed against the fence, trying his hand at roping with a lasso that was the perfect size for him.

Claire's entire body grew warm, and butterflies fluttered in her belly. Misty River wasn't the type of horse a man building a premier ranch needed to buy. Realizing he'd purchased the little mare for her children did funny things to her heart and made her brain buzz with thoughts she'd been promising herself she would not entertain.

Hugging the collar of her heavy sweater tightly against the cold, she forced herself to remember that the price of romantic fantasies was steep. Too steep. And yet, even as she warned herself not to confuse for now with forever, she felt some long-fearful part of her relaxing, laying down its weapons of defense and softening into life.

"That's just another way of saying you're becoming reckless," she whispered to herself and shivered.

From the time she was little, she'd imagined being part of a "real" family someday, and she'd lived that dream for eight years. Since her husband's passing, she'd told herself over and over that those years were something to be grateful for, and satisfied with. She'd worked hard at replacing the picture of mommy, daddy and kids that she'd carried so long in her mind with a new mental snapshot depicting a single mother happily raising three children in a loving home and supportive community. She'd forcefully envisioned herself carving the Thanksgiving turkey, removing the cookies left for Santa Claus and standing proudly at her babies' high school graduations, her single presence enough for them and for her.

But now...

Claire looked at the scene in the corral, remembered the afternoons of sheer passion and the nights Fletcher dedicated to her self-improvement, and her vision blurred. The future looked fuzzy now without him in it. Then she dropped the loner cowboy into the picture in her mind and—bang! It cleared right up.

This was bad. Very bad.

True love had ruined her mother, each failed attempt at happily-ever-after weakening Didi like a pair of scissors clipping her muscles until she couldn't stand on her own anymore. No child should be made to live under the weight of a parent's dashed dreams.

Allowing raw fear to propel her, Claire ran to the hall closet for her coat. It was time to wrap up the morning. She needed time away from Fletcher, time and the distance to put her relationship with him in its proper perspective. They were having a casual affair—the first and, if her nauseous stomach and sweaty palms were any indication, the last one of her life.

Grabbing her old trench coat off a hanger, she whipped it out of the small closet, pausing when she heard something clatter to the floor. Stepping back, she bent to retrieve Fletcher's wooden cane then realized that she hadn't seen him use it in several days. As she pulled the intricately patterned stick from the closet to set it aright again, her eyes widened.

A carved wooden horse's head replaced the original curved handle.

*A horse's head.*

The night Fletcher had joined her family for a movie, he'd asked her whether Will enjoyed playing "horses" or whether he did it only to appease Orlando. She had responded that Will liked it more than Orlando, and that she was hoping to buy him his own hobbyhorse for Christmas.

Fletcher had made the beautiful toy for her son, a child who rarely asked for anything anymore, because he was so busy trying to be the man of the house.

For a long while she held the horse, uncertainty making her sick. Wasn't love supposed to cast out fear? If so, it wasn't working. Because here she was, filled from head to toe by a churning apprehension even as she realized that what she felt for Fletcher might not be mere passion or gratitude or infatuation, but something much deeper and more dangerous.

## Chapter Twelve

"The mayor is in a meeting with Pastor Skidmore from the Methodist church over on D Street. There's a vacant lot next door that turns into a sinkhole every winter, and the UMC wants it for a parking lot." The receptionist at city hall shook her head, thin coral-tinted lips pursed. "That's waving a red flag in front of the Almighty, if you ask my opinion, because everyone knows there's been water under that land for a hundred years or more. Can't you see the cars being sucked into the earth on a Sunday morning? That is the kind of publicity I would avoid if I was running a church, I can tell you…."

With tightly permed hair springing from her scalp in artificially gold coils, the woman whose nameplate read "Miss Vivian Reynolds" kept talking while Fletcher waited for the answer to his question: "Can I get an appointment with the mayor?"

Gesturing to the garage-sale green leather chair stationed

by the front window, Fletcher interrupted to tell her, "I'll wait until he's through."

Vivian nodded. "Oh. Okeydoke. He who?"

"The mayor."

She laughed, showing wide, white teeth. "The mayor is a woman. It's a new millennium, honey." She shook her head. "Men. Oh, my goodness."

While Vivian no doubt added Fletcher's gaffe to the collection of anecdotes she could take to her next hair appointment, he took a seat, entertaining himself with an old issue of *Portland Monthly*. He felt remarkably calm under the circumstances.

When he'd first learned that his father's will mandated marriage or the forfeiture of Pine Road Ranch to Honeyford, he had anticipated a showdown of Old West proportions, punctuated by as many threats as it took until the city agreed to sell him the house and property that were his birthright. Fletcher had returned to Honeyford geared up for battle. Only a few weeks ago, he'd have burned the ranch to the ground before he'd have agreed to a marriage of convenience. Now the rage inside him had waned. And he knew exactly why.

Images of Claire—at her house, on the ranch, in his bed— nearly made him put the magazine down, bag the meeting with the mayor and head home, where she was, no doubt, listening to a book on tape (her habit of late) as she worked.

After this weekend, he felt less anxious about the ranch. It seemed a given now that he would reclaim it. He'd worked like a fiend since the start of November, readying the barn and corrals and mending fencing. With the arrival of his first horses, he could envision the ranch exactly the way he wanted it to be.

At the age of twenty-eight, he was a self-made man, with rodeo buckles and commercial endorsements and a financial portfolio men twice his age might envy. But this past weekend marked the first time in his adult life that he had experienced true satisfaction.

His lips curved as he pictured the sheer joy on Orlando's face and the concentration on Will's as they rode around the corral on Misty River. Claire had phoned Sunday morning to say that Orlando and Will played "rodeo riders" until bedtime Saturday night, with Will riding the hobbyhorse Fletcher had fashioned from his cane. As long as Fletcher lived, he would not forget the way Will looked at him when he realized the wooden horse with the intricately carved stick was all his. With Will blinking at him in awe, Fletcher had glanced up for a second, and his eyes had met Claire's.

Rodeo fans had asked for his autograph. Interviewers had recorded his thoughts in print and on tape. Once, he'd seen his own face on the side of a bus. None of those milestone accomplishments had relieved him of the persistent sense that he was a failure at life. Then he'd glanced up, saw Claire looking at him with her heart in her eyes and he'd felt like a hero.

He wanted the ranch, but suddenly vengeance was the furthest thing from his mind.

Wind splattered droplets of rain against the window behind him. The heater in the old cottage that housed city hall kicked in, noisily warming the reception area, and Fletcher leafed through the issue of *Portland Monthly,* beginning to feel excited by the idea of taking Claire and the kids to Portland for a weekend vacation, maybe to watch the Christmas tree lighting in Pioneer Square.

Down the hallway to his left, a door opened. Footsteps on wood flooring and the sound of voices turned Fletcher's attention to Vivian, who said, "Here comes the mayor. Let's see if she has any time."

Setting aside the magazine, Fletcher rose, prepared to insist on at least a five-minute audience. Without rage fueling him, he could be persuaded to schedule a later meeting after he introduced himself to the mayor and discovered exactly whom he should approach about buying the property.

He even experimented with a consciously friendly expression as the mayor and her current guests entered the area in front of the reception desk.

"Well, thank you, Madam Mayor." The older of the two gentlemen shook the middle-aged woman's hand. "*A Honeyford Christmas* is guaran*damn*teed to bring in tourist dollars, and I know the community theater is going to appreciate your appearance at our opening night."

"It'll be my pleasure, Burt. I certainly look forward to seeing the play." Poised, elegant and far more citified than one would expect of the mayor in a town that was still as rustic as Honeyford, the mayor gestured to the receptionist she shared with the other denizens of city hall. "Give Vivian the details, and she'll put it on my calendar."

"Gotcha," the receptionist said. "As long as I can come, too. I hear there's going to be a champagne reception. That beats the coffee and doughnuts you served after *On Golden Pond*." Vivian guffawed happily. "You've got someone waiting for you, Gwen." Stabbing her pen in Fletcher's direction, she tucked a pair of rhinestone-studded glasses on her face then addressed her attention to a large appointment book.

The mayor turned toward Fletcher, her smile ready, her well-heeled feet already moving in his direction.

Fletcher stood rooted to the spot. The equilibrium he'd enjoyed only moments before disappeared like vapor, replaced by a fury that felt more familiar.

Gwen Gibson faltered only a bit as she recognized her visitor. The smile on her face wobbled, but did not disappear. Rather than stretching out her right hand, however, she twined it with her left, the only outward sign of discomposure. "I hoped you'd come see me."

One breath. Two. Fletcher struggled for calm when every cell in his body felt like a match striking flint. No words formed in his brain. The puzzling pieces of his father's will began to fall into place. Victor wasn't giving *Honeyford* the ranch; he was giving it to Gwen.

Gwen Gibson. Once his mother's best friend, her presence in the Kingsleys' lives had ultimately turned love to bitterness and robbed the family of their future together. Fletcher hadn't seen Gwen for eighteen years, not since the day she'd approached him to offer her condolences over his mother's tragic death.

He felt his heart pounding, his fists clenching. Fletcher had never even asked where his father was buried. Now he wanted to find the grave and vent his outrage.

"Why don't we speak in my office?" Gwen's modulated tone shook him from his silent wrath.

His lips parted like a beast about to devour its prey. "I'll pass."

The words emerged raw and choked. Too revealing. He struggled to find the kiss-my-ass insolence of his youth before he spoke again. "Call me old-fashioned," he added, going for the kill, "but I don't see much benefit in becoming reacquainted with my father's mistress."

He pivoted, swallowing the two feet between him and the door. He opened it, allowing the winter storm to attack the entry as he added, "About Victor's will—the day I let you have my mother's ranch will be the day I'm lowered into *my* grave. My lawyer will be in touch."

Fletcher drove for an hour before returning to the ranch. When he pulled up to the house, he parked next to Claire's Oldsmobile and a late-model Hybrid sedan.

Smoke rose lazily from the chimney, the porch was swept and a collection of Thanksgiving-themed decorations dressed his front door. Claire had been hard at work, readying his home for holiday memories. This morning he would have appreciated the effort. Now he knew it was wasted. Ghosts haunted Pine Road Ranch, and they weren't going to relocate because one small woman tried to scrub them away.

Walking heavily up the steps, he opened the front door, where he found his brother sitting on the sofa, a mug of coffee on the table in front of him. Dean rose as soon as he saw Fletcher.

"Where's Claire?" Fletcher shut the door behind him, feeling the beginnings of a massive headache.

"She's in the kitchen."

Recognizing the aroma of fresh bread did little to improve Fletcher's mood. "What are you doing here?"

Neatly and conservatively dressed for work, Dean nonetheless appeared unusually disheveled, as if he'd been running his hands through his hair. Carefully, he responded, "I heard you met with Gwen."

Fletcher stared at his half brother, his blood a cold river in his veins. "Well, doesn't that beat all?" He removed his jacket, hanging it on the coat tree while he stemmed the urge to throw Dean out on his ass. Facing the man he had once considered too perfect, Fletcher glared, devoid of respect. "My brother is friends with our father's mistress. How long has this been going on? Or have you two been chummy through the years?"

Dean was no fool; he knew better than to try to diffuse Fletcher's volatility. Instead, he replied simply, "Gwen returned to Honeyford a few years ago, after she was widowed. Nothing went on again between her and Dad—"

Fletcher strode across the hardwood floor. "The damage was done twenty years ago when 'Aunt' Gwen hopped into bed with her best friend's husband."

"They were wrong, and they paid for it—"

"They paid for it? *They* did? How's that, Deano? They stopped seeing each other for a week after my mother's funeral?"

Dean ran his hands through his hair, further disrupting its customary neat style. He started to respond then looked to his right. Fletcher followed his gaze and saw Claire, standing on the edge of the living room, watching him with concerned eyes. "I came in to say I made lunch, but…" Changing her mind, she pointed toward the kitchen. "I'll be in the—"

"No!" Fletcher held out a hand. "Stay. You might as well hear the truth. This house is haunted, Claire. Can you feel it? There are ghosts everywhere."

Dean shook his head. "Don't drag her into this—"

"Drag her in?" Fletcher laughed, but the sound was ugly. "I'm going to tell her everything she needs to know so she can run." He'd planned to come back here today and persuade Claire to ignore work in favor of getting naked. She'd been resisting that lately, claiming their relationship would be a conflict of interests with her job unless they confined their lovemaking to after hours. He'd been thinking up all sorts of ways to convince her otherwise. Now he looked at the woman who had made him feel, if only for a short while, alive and clean and very nearly whole again. He shook his head. Family. Future. For her, it was reality; for him, an illusion.

"Sit down, Claire." Walking to a leather wingback chair, he seated himself and waited while Dean and Claire cautiously took their places on the sofa. He looked first at Dean, with a grim, leveled gaze that made clear he would leave nothing out of this story. Then he faced Claire, his heart gripping as it struggled vainly to hang on to the tender feelings reborn since he'd known her. *Let it go. Let her go.* He started talking.

"When I was a kid, this was a working horse ranch. It didn't look the way it does now. There wasn't an inch of fencing out of order. The house was painted so white it glowed.

My grandfather owned and ran the spread. My mother and I lived here with him." Fletcher glanced at his brother. "For a while Dean and our father, Victor, did, too. Dean and I have different mothers. Did I mention that before?"

Claire felt unsure of how to respond. From the moment Dean had arrived at the ranch, concerned and agitated, she had realized that Fletcher was in some sort of trouble. Dean's discretion seemed to suggest it was a private matter, so she'd given him coffee and let him wait in the living room while she tried to calm her worry in the kitchen.

Looking at Fletcher now, Claire longed to touch him, to peel away the burdens he wore like multiple layers of skin.

"I know your father was widowed before he moved to Honeyford," she responded carefully.

"By all accounts, Victor and Dean's mother were a love affair. Right, Deano?"

Claire glanced to her left, but Dean's gaze remained fixed on Fletcher. For the first time since she'd met him, the gentle pharmacist was silent and foreboding.

"My mother and Victor weren't so lucky," Fletcher continued. "She was happiest on the ranch. Comfortable. Free. Living in town suffocated her. Small towns love their local doctor like they love their local pharmacist. We had to be on our best behavior, but my mother never managed to conform to Victor's standard." From the corner of her eye, Claire saw Dean shake his head. Fletcher either missed the gesture or ignored it.

"Jule, my mother, was unconventional," he continued. "She embarrassed Victor. Fortunately my mother had a good friend who sympathized with her. Have you met Gwen Gibson yet, Claire? She's the mayor."

Claire nodded. "She buys muffins for her staff every Monday."

Fletcher's eyes turned hard as flint; irony gnawed into

his words. "She was always a generous woman. My mother referred to Gwen as a soul sister. In fact, I used to call her 'Aunt.'"

Claire's stomach curdled with apprehension. The mayor had emerged from her office to greet her with much graciousness and welcome the first time Claire had peddled her baked goods to city hall.

"Jule became so miserable in town that Victor agreed to let us come back to the ranch," Fletcher continued. "Without him. Dean had left for college by then, so Victor sold the house we'd been living in and moved into an apartment above the pharmacy." Fletcher leaned back, linking his hands over his beltline. Claire heard his knuckles crack. "In the past when we were at the ranch Jule was happy. Not this time. She stayed in her room during the day. Wouldn't get dressed. She had outbursts of anger that seemed to come out of nowhere. Then one morning, my grandfather found her wandering in the rain at five a.m. She'd hadn't been to bed." Fletcher's knuckles grew white as he clenched his fists. "She cried all that day and the next. So I decided to pay my father a visit and tell him what was going on."

Unable to sit any longer, Fletcher rose and paced to the hearth. Fire and tension crackled in the warm room. "I'm not sure what I expected. By that time, I knew damned well that Victor viewed my mother as a burden, and I half hated him already, but hope dies hard when you're a kid. So I hitched a ride to town one evening with someone who worked for my grandfather, and I went to Victor's apartment. I used the alley entrance. I was going to beg him to move back to the ranch. I honest-to-God thought I was going to throw up as I climbed the stairs."

Fletcher looked up, making contact with Claire, and when she read the despair in his eyes, she longed to erase his pain. She knew better, though. As someone who'd survived her own distressed childhood, she understood intimately that at some point the battle had to be waged inside rather than out. So she perched on the edge of his sofa, anxious but still, and put her heart in her gaze as she waited for the rest of the story.

"I was about to knock on the door. Then I saw a movement through the window. Victor was in there. With Gwen. They were holding each other. I wasn't quite nine, but it didn't take much experience to know it wasn't a platonic hug. I watched a little longer and then I pounded so hard on the window it broke."

He turned to stare at the flames. "They shouted. I ran. Victor showed up at the ranch that night, and I heard him talking to Jule in her bedroom. She'd known about Gwen all along. He went back to town, and my mother…got crazier. I don't think we had a normal day after that, but we began to learn to live with the status quo. Then my grandfather had a massive heart attack. Within a week of the funeral, Victor came to the ranch to tell Jule and me to pack up, we were going to be moving back to town with him."

Beside her, Claire saw Dean lower his head. Gone was the relaxed, easy-going man she had come to appreciate. The muscles along Dean's jaw bunched as if he were chewing. His forehead furrowed.

She returned her attention to Fletcher, who had been her lover and her friend for a treasured collection of days and nights, and understood for the first time the enormity of the lie she'd been telling herself.

Last night, studying for her GED, she had come across the word "oxymoron." "A combination of contradictory words" was the dictionary definition, and she'd written several examples for her workbook. Now she had the best example of all: simple relationship.

Like the one she'd wanted to have with Fletcher.

The pain in the living room of this once grand family

home was turning into a living thing, a current that pulsed between the brothers and turned the air thick and useless. If it affected Fletcher, it affected her. She and Fletcher did not exist in an isolated present, no matter how they pretended. She had tried to tell herself he was her fantasy cowboy, and that they would both be okay when the time came to walk toward their separate sunsets. She'd pretended her heart and his would remain safe. But the moment a heart started pumping, it put itself in harm's way. Now his pain was hers.

Apprehension filled her with heat as Fletcher spoke again, his tone blunt and steely, a weapon he turned on himself.

"I told Victor to go to hell, that Jule and I were staying. He said she couldn't care for herself anymore, much less herself and a kid, so I told him I'd take care of us, and who the hell was he to judge anyone's parenting? Jule started crying, and I—" With a smirk of self-disgust, Fletcher rubbed his eyes. "I ran Victor off with my grandfather's shotgun. Victor phoned every day to try to talk Jule into moving, but she'd become hysterical, and I'd grab the phone and hang up on him. I believed I could do it—take care of my mother, stay on the ranch, make things the way they used to be." He shook his head. "Hell, I could barely remember the way they used to be."

Dean rose and crossed to the window, where he stood looking out. Fletcher gave no indication he was watching his brother and continued the story in a monotone. "Jule's anxiety seemed to double every day. By the end of the week, she wasn't eating, refused food...I don't think she slept at all. She'd talk about moving to town, but then seem tortured by the possibility. I cut school a few times that week, but by Friday I went back just to get away. I hung out, wasted time, came home as late as I dared. When I got here, Jule was gone. I couldn't find her anywhere, so I searched the ranch."

The words grew clipped, his tone rough and full of effort. "I found her in the barn. She'd hanged herself."

Claire felt nausea rise to her throat. She wanted to run to Fletcher, lay her head against his chest and throw her arms around his body, a human fence to shield him from further pain. But Fletcher stood rigid as a mountain, his face hard as granite, and determined. "I cut her down and phoned Victor," he said in the same chilling monotone. "He handled things, then gave me a choice between foster care and moving in with him. So I moved in and dedicated myself to making him miserable until the day I left."

His eyes were dry and hollow when he looked at Claire. "My grandfather willed this ranch to my mother. Her will left everything to Victor."

Claire felt as if her brain were spinning inside her head. She could hardly fathom the pain of a child seeing what he had seen, and now...what was he saying? "But Pine Road Ranch is yours now. Isn't it?"

After facing away from each other during the most wrenching part of Fletcher's story, he and Dean connected, their gazes challenging. Fletcher opened his mouth to respond to Claire, but Dean jumped in. "Our father's will specifies marriage as a prerequisite to claim our inheritances."

"In English," Fletcher clarified, "that's 'Marry or else.'"

"I don't understand." Claire's stomach churned as rapidly as her mind. "You're living here. You have keys."

"I broke in," Fletcher said. "And changed the locks."

Her mouth went dry. "So you have to marry to legally inherit your ranch, and if you don't?"

"The will states that the property goes to Honeyford."

*And Gwen Gibson, their father's mistress, was the mayor of the town.* For the life of her, Claire could not comprehend why Fletcher's father would do such a thing. She understood better why seeing Gwen today upset him so. And then she realized something else.

"How long have you known about the will?"

The expression on Fletcher's face told her he understood exactly what she was asking.

He turned to Dean. "Thanks for coming, but you need to leave now. There are things I have to discuss with Claire. Alone."

Dean looked at her without bothering to mask his surprise. As far as she knew, it was his first inkling that she shared more than an employee-employer relationship with his brother.

If Dean disapproved, he didn't show it. Neither did he ask questions. The gentleman slipped behind the handsome face once more, and he merely nodded before making his way to the front door.

"I'd like to talk to you before you see Gwen again," he requested quietly of Fletcher.

Shrugging, Fletcher kept his expression as neutral as Dean's, though it was arguably less congenial.

The door closed behind Dean, and Claire didn't know whether to be relieved or nervous now that she could speak more freely in front of Fletcher.

"If you want to run for the hills right now, before you hear me out, you do it," he said before she had a chance to gather her scattered thoughts. "I'm sure as hell not judging. But I want to tell you one thing."

Claire ignored the rush of anger his suggestion engendered. "Go ahead."

"What happened between you and me has nothing to do with the will. I wasn't thinking about marriage…. I'm not going to get married."

Unable to sit any longer, Claire rose. She took a breath, made sure she was steady on her feet after being pelted with so many facts and then walked toward him. Fletcher's expression morphed slowly from stony to wary as she made her way across his living room.

"I'm glad you said that, about our relationship having nothing to do with the will," she said when she was close enough to touch him if she wanted to. "I wouldn't want to be manipulated, and I don't know what your daddy was thinking. No one should be forced into marriage."

"I should have told you the rest of it before." In the brief gap between her words and his, Fletcher relaxed his guard then snapped it into place again. "You don't want to entangle your life with mine." His voice sounded as hard as the armor he hid himself beneath. "You can work here as long as you need to, until you find something else. Something better. I'll stay out of your way."

Claire shook her head as if that would clear the perplexing tangle of thoughts. "You want me to work for you…and that's all? You really think we can go backwards like that?"

"We never should have gone forward." His lips barely moved.

"Are you saying this because you're having second thoughts about me, or because you think I'm having second thoughts about you?"

Fletcher scowled. He thumped his fist once against the fireplace mantel. "You damn well better be having second thoughts about me. What happens to a horse when it breaks a leg, Claire?"

She shook her head in confusion. "What are you asking?"

His black hair and dark expression gave him a menacing air as he took a step forward and loomed over her. "Think. A horse lives on its legs. If the break is bad enough, you put the horse down. You don't try to fix it."

"I still don't—"

"I haven't cared about anything but revenge for twenty years. It's what I care about now. The past two weeks were a memory lapse for me. That's all. I am who I am, Claire. Something broke inside me a long time ago, and there's no fixing it. And I'm all through pretending. I've got business to attend to." He smiled grimly. Sadly. "So the you-and-me portion of our program…is officially concluded."

Straightening away from her, Fletcher looked over her head, past her, though his eyes were empty and unfocused. "Take the rest of the day off. You can work here as long as you need to, like I said, but I want you to start looking for a new job."

"I don't need to start looking for a new job. I already have one."

Claire's statement, gritty and matter-of-fact, caught him off guard. She allowed herself a moment of satisfaction.

"Henry Berns at the bakery offered me a full-time job yesterday. Irene told him about me. The hours aren't ideal, but I'll be doing something I love with a chance to become a partner someday if I can save enough money. I already told him I'd take it." She let the information settle, watching him carefully. "It's become clear anyway that working here and having a relationship with you puts us in a difficult spot. It's not good for your reputation or mine."

Fletcher nodded slowly, still without looking at her. His jaw was clenched, his brow tense and furrowed. He said nothing, but his Adam's apple bobbed once as he swallowed.

He wasn't going to wage the smallest battle for his freedom. Claire wanted to shake him. "You're not a horse, you know. I learned about metaphors this week in my language arts book, and that's a bad one. You're a…" She looked him up and down. "…a whipped dog. The kind that goes back to its master for more beating instead of finding a new home." She had his full attention now. Taking a breath to steady herself, she pressed on, sensing she had one shot to knock him off the path he was on, the one that was going to put an end to them tonight. "You hang on to that past of yours as if it's the hand that feeds you. As if it's all that's real. It's not. I'm real, too, Fletcher."

They were less than a yard apart, but he was looking at her as if she were crazy, as if she were speaking a language he'd never heard before and couldn't begin to understand. Obviously words would not be enough.

The space between them was either two feet or a chasm, depending on the point of view. Claire figured she could tiptoe across it or jump.

"I was going to give you two weeks' notice." She dropped her voice and lowered her chin, looking at him from under her lashes. "Now I've changed my mind. I quit. Today. This second." Closing the distance between them, she held his gaze. "I don't work for you anymore, Mr. Kingsley, and that means…" She raised her hands to his chest. "…I could spend the rest of the afternoon touching you, and it wouldn't be a conflict of interests at all."

He reacted as if her touch burned, grabbing her wrists and holding her away.

"Why can't you understand? There's no future here." His low growl rose from the center of his body. "Not with me."

His words had an effect. Claire felt something tweak inside her, like a guitar string snapping, but she couldn't examine it now. She'd told herself from the beginning that the relationship between her and Fletcher was a gift to hold for a while, not something that would last forever.

"You jump to too many conclusions," she told him, wishing he'd let go so she could smooth the worried wrinkles from his brow. "If you're not looking back, then you're trying to see over everyone's heads into the future. Look at me, Fletcher." Her voice fell to a whisper. "Look at *me*. I'm here. Right now.

And I'm not asking you to take care of me. Let me take care of you. Just for now."

She felt his grip loosening and moved her hands to his face. With her palms on his cheeks, she rose to her toes and kissed him gently. Feeling him stiffen and start to pull away, Claire moved one hand to the nape of his neck, the other to his chest and deepened the kiss—the way he'd taught her.

Slowly, as if he moved against his own will, Fletcher gave in, releasing her arms and gripping her hips, her back, holding her like a man at sea who'd bumped into a lifeboat, as if she were all that lay between him and drowning.

He tried to say something else, something that sounded like a final plea for her to run away, but Claire refused to listen. Or to let go. Today she would love him as he deserved to be loved—as the boy whose heart had been broken and the man who'd lost his way. Fletcher was as big and complex and messy as life itself, and Claire felt every cell in her body wake up when they were together. He was the danger she had warned herself against, igniting the yearnings she had told herself not to feel.

Tomorrow she could play it safe. Today, Fletcher required more than distraction; he needed her loving.

Wrapping her arms like a cocoon around him, she gave her whole self to this man who made hobbyhorses for fatherless boys and tutored uneducated women, but didn't know how to forgive the past. She gave herself to his need, to her own yearning.

"I can't."

Two words. Whispered. Chilling.

And very final.

Claire might have attempted to ignore them, but the hands that seconds ago had pulled her in now pushed her away. She watched his eyes fill then dry again before a single tear fell. His eyes, his beautiful gray eyes—so stormy, so perceptive—looked like a desolate sky, too tired even to rain. A protest rose inside her, but almost imperceptibly he shook his head.

He may have said he was sorry; Claire wasn't sure. For the longest time after he walked away all she heard clearly was the thunder of pain. His, so desperate and deep. And hers, the pain of a woman who had gone back on her word and had fallen in love with a dangerous man.

## Chapter Thirteen

In the calm of rainless winter twilight, a bulge of smoke, acrid and portentous, filled the sky above the house on Pine Road Ranch. Fletcher stood back, a metal gasoline container by his feet, his gaze trained on the blaze he'd started moments before.

There was a wrestling match inside him, thoughts and feelings grappling with no respect for rules or civility. Vengeance, against his father and Gwen and perhaps against life itself, occupied the lion's share of his mind, burning its seal onto his brain cells, just as it had in his youth. But his heart...

Not for the first time that night, Fletcher felt a physical pain that threatened to double him over. After seeing Gwen and realizing that his father's mistress was somehow implicated in the travesty of the will, Fletcher had been certain his rage would bully any gentler emotions into fleeing. His heart might be full of Claire and her children now, but how long would that last? How long before his rage spilled over onto everyone and everything around him as it always had? And, how could he possibly be the man those four deserved?

The answer was obvious: he couldn't. Still, the tension between his past and his present refused to calm.

Last week Claire had gone through boxes in the attic. She'd found several with items belonging to Victor, cheap, mostly inconsequential things his father either hadn't found it necessary to move to the city or which his mother had kept as mementos. There were boxes of Fletcher's old things, too, including baseball bats and mitts that were worn thin, and with them came memories he'd buried a lifetime ago. He and Victor had once played ball in this very yard.

Merely knowing the boxes were in the house became too much to take tonight. Ironically, he longed for the clarity of the days when his hatred was pure, no softer feelings to dilute it. So tonight he had decided to burn the memories.

The cardboard boxes he'd piled in the yard behind the house dissolved easily on the tongues of the flames. The other items were slower to disintegrate. He waited. Controlled burns took time.

The noise from the crackling fire and his own querulous thoughts masked the arrival of a car out front. Fletcher didn't realize he had company until a woman raced around the side of the house, stumbling in her haste to reach him.

"What are you doing? Get back! You're going to be hurt!"

She yanked on his arm, shouting warnings until he grabbed her shoulders and moved them both back by several yards. Gwen Gibson stared at him, wild-eyed. Realizing he was still holding her, he released her shoulders as if they were hotter than the fire he'd started.

As always, she was dressed handsomely in a slim skirt, blouse and blazer. Conservative, attractive, in control. So different from his more flamboyant, more unpredictable mother.

Looking at the fire, she shuddered. "When I saw the smoke, I thought—"

Fletcher smiled grimly and completed the sentence. "That I was burning the house down? I thought about it. Then I realized Victor would probably appreciate that."

Her well-arched brows drew together, but she chose not to comment, asking instead, "Do you have that thing under control?"

On the verge of making a smart-ass comment, Fletcher controlled himself to say, "I know what I'm doing."

"What are you burning?"

He looked at her. Would the knowledge that he was burning articles once belonging to her lover be hurtful? Did she still care? Three years after finding her with his father, Fletcher had heard that Gwen married and moved to Lane County. "What brought you back to Honeyford?" he asked abruptly.

She seemed to know what he was truly asking, even before he did. "My husband passed away a few years ago. I was working for the city of Eugene, but my hours were cut, and I welcomed the opportunity to get my daughter out of the city, so I moved back to Honeyford. I didn't come back because of your father." She watched him carefully. "Returning to the scene of the crime. Is that what you're thinking?"

Fletcher shrugged. Once she'd been "Aunt Gwen." He'd have played with her kid as if they were blood relations. "Do you really care what I'm thinking?"

"Yes, I do. I've tried to make that clear over the years." She smoothed the thick paper wrapping of the package she held. "Victor and I ended our affair the evening you found us. I've tried to get in touch over the years to explain this to you because it's important to me that you understand. Your father was the love of my life." She raised her chin, keeping her gaze steady. "And I believe I was that for him. But we both understood how horribly we hurt you—and Jule—so we put that part of our lives behind us. We hadn't spoken in years before I returned home. When he heard I was back, he got in touch. By then, he suspected he didn't have long to live."

At the shock Fletcher couldn't disguise, Gwen's expression turned compassionate. Firelight illuminated her face. "He didn't want you to know. You or Dean. He'd been on heart medication for some time. He went to a pharmacy in Bend to fill the prescription so Dean wouldn't worry, but he continued to have dangerous fibrillations, and as a physician he knew anything could happen. He knew he had unfinished business, so he came up with that terrible condition in his will."

Gwen had Fletcher's full attention now. The mere mention of the will sent his blood pressure skyward.

"If it's any consolation, I think forcing you and Dean to consider marriage was the act of a very desperate man."

"Desperate?" Now Fletcher knew Gwen was reacting more from emotion than reason. "Victor?" His father had possessed an almost eerie calm. Provoking Victor to anger, to anything, had been one of Fletcher's treasured pastimes.

For the first time, Gwen looked at Fletcher with disappointment. "Is it so hard to imagine that your father might have had strong feelings about the circumstances in his life? About the kind of father he'd been?" She lowered her voice as if afraid of inciting him, but she persisted. "About the kind of husband he'd been? He'd influenced two sons to reject intimate relationships like the plague. The sins of the father." She shook her head, her sadness immense. "Victor was terrified he'd poisoned you and Dean against marriage for life. And yet he knew, Fletcher—" she took a breath and spoke more strongly "—he knew that no life could reach its full potential without love."

There was so much to say, so many poison-tipped arrows to launch at that particular target, that Fletcher didn't trust himself to speak.

Gwen raised the package in her hands. "This is yours. I tried a couple of times to send it to you, but it came back." Pushing it toward him, her gaze flickered toward his bonfire. "I hope this time you'll open it."

Gwen had sent him cards, too, over the years, on holidays, presumably to make amends, and Fletcher had dealt with them the same way he'd handled the package: return to sender. For the first time, his conscience pricked him. Reluctantly accepting the parcel, he questioned, "What's in it?"

She smiled. "You know, I believe I've exercised my courage all I can for one evening. I'll leave you to find out for yourself. Just remember to keep an open mind, please. I'm not trying to shift blame. I take full responsibility for what your father and I did. But perhaps understanding will help you to forgive. Yourself and us."

Gwen pivoted quickly then, her pumps sinking awkwardly in the uneven soil. Fletcher watched her, frowning. Within a few feet, she stopped, turned and looked back. "You don't want to hear this now, I know. But if you ever want to talk— about anything—I'm here."

She left, and Fletcher stood where he was, listening for her car as it traveled along the dirt driveway. Once Gwen was gone, the box she'd left with him felt hotter than the fire. He did not open it, however, until the controlled burn had spent itself, and he was inside the house again, a whiskey-laced coffee at his elbow.

Anxiety was not a sensation Fletcher had felt often as an adult. He preferred to bully his fear with anger or indifference.

But now, as he stared at the package, not much larger than a shoebox, he felt his heartbeat accelerate and perspiration dot his upper lip. His whole body buzzed.

All he'd gleaned from Gwen's sketchy explanation was that the contents of this box had something to do with her and his father. That information alone should have compelled him to toss the damn thing into the flames, but something stopped him.

No mere burning of objects could solve his dilemma; that had become apparent tonight.

Claire and her kids changed everything.

Pulling his hand from the mug, he rubbed his face. For so long his heart had been filled with the weeds of anger and cynicism, too thick to allow anything else to grow. Claire had sewn seeds of love that were struggling to take root, but their battle to survive felt like it was killing him.

*Keep an open mind,* Gwen had said. He had nothing left to lose.

Tearing the paper from the package, he opened the lid on a plain white box. A collection of books, some clothbound and some leather, lay neatly stacked inside. It took a moment to realize the volumes were personal journals, and then Fletcher had to fight not to clamp the lid down again, trapping the ghosts of the past inside.

Removing one of the slim leather books, he swallowed the unreasonable fear collecting in his throat and opened the cover. Shock ran through him like an electric current. He had expected the journals to belong to his mother, but it was Victor's handwriting, neat and orderly, that filled the page.

Perspiration covered Fletcher's face and dampened his back as he scanned the first entry and began to understand what was at stake. Love or hatred—he could hold one, but not both at the same time. Gwen had put the choice in his hands.

Tonight he would find a way to believe Claire's garden

could grow inside him, or he would have a reason to throw down his spade and let the weeds take over once and for all.

"I know you'll enjoy the pecan rolls, Mrs. Celmer. I used the bakery's challah recipe for the dough and my own special combination of spices for the filling. You be sure to come back and tell Mr. Berns what you think."

Claire handed Mary Sue Celmer a pink box wrapped with twine, exactly the way Henry Berns had been boxing pastries at Honey Bea's Bakery for forty-some-odd years. Smiling at her customer, Claire hoped her cheerful expression successfully masked the sadness that pulled at her on the inside. Her new job as chief baker and hopeful future partner in the bakery required a level of fortitude she hadn't needed since right after Arlo's passing.

Losing Fletcher felt like another death.

"Dear girl." Henry's voice, gravelly, he claimed, from too many cigarillos in his youth, turned her around.

Smoothing a brown apron with pink stitching that read "Honey Bea's," Claire dredged up one more smile. "We completely sold out the pecan rolls, Mr. Berns," she told him, "and I doubt the *pogaches* will last through lunch."

"Good, good. Listen, *bubelah,* I've told you once, and I'm telling you again— My name is Henry, not 'Mr. Berns.' Or you can call me *Zayde* Henry like most everyone else in town."

"*Zayde?*"

"It means 'grandpa' in Yiddish. It's a very friendly word." He placed the skinny fingers of both hands on his chest. "And I'm a friendly person, right? Right. So you'll stop tiptoeing around me. Already I see that you're wonderful for business. My Miriam loves you."

Mr. Berns…Zayde Henry…consistently spoke of his late

wife as if she were still alive. Irene had told Claire that the couple had been inseparable and that Henry rarely went anywhere other than the bakery since Miriam's passing two years back.

Claire thanked him for the compliment. "It's almost eleven, so I think I'll make a few sandwiches to have ready for lunch."

Henry shrugged. "Sure. Take a break, too. Have you tried a *pogache* with a cup of ginger tea? Nothing better." Behind his gray mustache and beard, the elderly man smiled, urging her away from the display case. "I'll take over. We have a lot of ladies who come in at lunchtime just to flirt with me. It makes Miriam so mad." His chocolate eyes crinkled with mischief. "It's best that I'm out front or the women will be disappointed. Go on," he shooed. "Tea and a cookie or two first, then you can make your sandwiches."

Claire grinned, more spontaneously this time, as she realized again how very fortunate she was to have this job, this future for herself and her family. She could not, *absopositively* would not, let a little thing like heartbreak deflect her from her purpose.

Straightening her spine, literally and figuratively, she poured hot water into a mug, grabbed a tea bag and headed to the rear of the store. She'd sip her tea *while* she was making the sandwiches. Keeping busy would keep her sane.

It had been three days since Fletcher had told her their affair was finished. She had not told her sons yet that their outings to the ranch were over. Every afternoon, they asked when they would see the cowboy they had begun to hero worship. Even Will dropped his caution in favor of little-boy enthusiasm when Fletcher's name was mentioned now.

Claire blamed herself for the pain and confusion they were sure to feel.

Ripping open the tea bag and plunging it into the mug,

she let her shoulders slump in the privacy of the bakery's kitchen. The morning shift was long gone; she had the area all to herself and didn't have to wear her game face when what she was feeling was…rotten. Sad and idiotic and mad.

*Dogs get mad, people get angry,* her mother used to correct, but Claire figured she was animal mad today. Mad at Fletcher and mad at herself and mad at life for making passion and prudence completely incompatible.

One week ago, at her place, Fletcher had spent an hour teaching Orlando to tie knots in a rope. Then he'd spent an equal amount of time concentrating on Will's "one-cent collection," which was a bunch of common pennies her son had found on various sidewalks. He'd even read Rozzy a bedtime story.

After the children had gone to bed, Fletcher had concentrated on her, spectacularly.

And she had let herself fall.

That night, she had decided to trust a world that, after a perfectly sweet marriage and three beautiful children, had chosen to give her passion and a heart so full she didn't know how it could hold one more thing.

Maybe some day she would forgive such treachery, such hazardous teasing, but for now she was just plain mad at life.

"I'm never going to fall in love again," Claire warned the world, daring it to contradict her. She picked up a knife to slice kaiser rolls.

"'I'll Never Fall in Love Again,' Dionne Warwick, nineteen sixty-eight. Miriam and I saw her at a theater in California. I forget which one." Henry reminisced, poking his head into the kitchen. "'To Life! L'Chaim!'—that's another good song. From *Fiddler on the Roof.* We saw that on Broadway. There's someone here to see you." He disappeared again.

Claire stared after him. Trailing behind the conversation,

it took her a beat or two to head to the front of the store. She found Henry at the coffeemaker, measuring "good old Yuban" into a filter. Without turning, he pointed a knobby finger toward the window.

Her breath caught as if she'd stepped into an icy river. Silhouetted in the wide picture window, Fletcher looked through the glass to the street beyond. Before she could say a word, he turned.

If expressions had hands, his would have reached out to squeeze her heart. Loss and longing, as plain and bare as the winter elms, filled his eyes.

Claire steeled herself. "What are you doing here?" She didn't want to be sucked in again.

With a glance toward Henry, he asked, "Do you get a break? Some time so we can talk?" Raw and hopeful, his beautiful baritone raised prickles of alarm along her skin.

Her hesitation alerted the older man, who abandoned the coffeemaker and shuffled to the display case. "Who are you?" he asked, abandoning his manners.

"Fletcher Kingsley, Mr. Berns."

"Doc Kingsley's boy?"

"Yes, sir."

Henry's lips pursed beneath his mustache. "The one that was always in trouble back in the nineties?"

Claire's protective instinct went on alert, but Fletcher took no offense. Looking Henry Berns in the eye, he admitted, "Yes, sir."

"Are you still trouble?"

The question shot a brief flare of surprise through Fletcher's gaze. Resignation and the shadow of humor followed. "Yes, sir. Sometimes I can be."

"Are you going to give her any trouble?" Henry tilted his grayed head toward Claire. "Because if you are, you can beat it, right now. And don't give *me* problems, because I've got a rolling pin here with your name on it."

The thought of her employer's thin arms wielding a rolling pin as a weapon of defense urged Claire into the mix. "Fletcher's not going to give anyone problems, Zayde Henry. He's very respectful now." She placed a calming hand on the small man's shoulder. To Fletcher, she responded with all the poise in her power, "I'm working, and...I think we've said everything that needs saying." She was not her mama, God bless Didi's heart. Claire might have been willing to risk her own heart, but she would not sacrifice her children's.

The muscles along his jaw tensed. "I haven't said anything that needs saying." Fletcher shook his head in a silent lament. His next words were hard won. "You don't have a single reason to give me the time of day. I know that. I'm asking, anyway. Ten minutes, Claire. You don't have to say a word. Just ten minutes of listening, and then I'll leave." He acknowledged Henry. "No rolling pin required."

Claire almost told him he was wrong: she had plenty of reasons to hear him out, the best being the intensity of her desire to roll back the clock and continue as they'd been before. Unfortunately, that was also the best reason not to give in.

Henry shuffled closer and patted her arm. "This is interesting. Like an episode of *Days of Our Lives*." He lowered his gravelly voice. "He seems sincere, *bubelah*. Sometimes the best decision is to listen before you make one."

Fletcher couldn't hide his surprise. Claire stared at the old man. With an impassive expression and a small nod, he told her he'd back any choice she made. Standing only a couple of inches taller than she and weighing about the same, he made her feel, for the first time in her life, a father's protection. If she made a mistake and fell, it wouldn't hurt any less, but she wouldn't be alone getting back up.

With her heart in her mouth, she nodded to Fletcher. "Ten minutes."

The door to the bakery opened, and Lucy Simms, the organist at Honeyford Presbyterian Church, entered, chatting with another woman.

Claire felt a second soft pat on her forearm. "Use the kitchen. You'll have privacy." Henry turned toward the women. "Ladies! You're in time for fresh coffee and chocolate chip *babke*. Take a seat." He motioned for Fletcher to step around the counter, and the six-foot-tall cowboy joined Claire.

"This way," she murmured, setting off immediately for the rear of the store in the hope he would not notice that the closer he got, the more heated and flushed her body became. It had been only a few days since she'd seen him, and she missed the way he politely nodded hello first then thoroughly kissed her when she arrived at his place in the morning. She missed the silly smile that rose from her heart and planted itself on her face when he knocked on her door in the evenings. She missed the way he made love.

Most of all, she missed living in a cloud of sweet daydreams.

*Slice the rolls.*

Taking herself to the table where she'd planned to assemble sandwiches, Claire got to work. Ten minutes of concentrating on food prep while he spoke couldn't be that tortuous, could it?

She kept her head down, but when the only sound she heard was the knife sawing through a kaiser roll, tension made her snap, "The clock is ticking, Mr. Kingsley."

She felt him move closer, but jumped anyway when his big hand closed over hers. Swallowing hard, she said, "I'm holding a knife. You shouldn't do that."

His palm was warm; his voice, whiskey and brown sugar.

"Ten minutes isn't much. Let me make the most of it." Gently, he slipped the knife from her fingers and set it aside. Then he turned her from the butcher-block counter so that she was facing him.

The desire to melt into his touch reminded her to do exactly the opposite. She stiffened. The soft bakery smells existed in direct contrast to the crackling anxiety inside her. She stepped back, putting several more inches between them.

"Okay." He nodded, accepting her need to protect herself. "So here goes. I've made more mistakes than any dozen human beings ought to in a lifetime. I sent you away in part because I didn't want to louse things up with you and the boys and Rozzy. Then Gwen came over and showed me that when it comes to lousing things up, I'm even better at it than I thought."

Claire felt a troublesome burst of protectiveness that seemed determined to kick in where Fletcher was concerned. "What did she tell you?"

Removing his heavy jacket, he hung it over the back of a barstool Henry perched on when he cut cookies.

"She brought me a box of things she took from my father's home after he died. They'd been out of touch for years, apparently, but reconnected when she moved back." He shook his head, rueful and self-deriding. "The fact that they'd reconnected would have bugged the crap out of me a few days ago."

"And it doesn't now?"

"Let's say it disturbs me in a different way than it would have before. The box she gave me was filled with journals, all handwritten, dated as far back as nineteen eighty-five. And all written by my father."

Given his feelings about his father, Claire showed what she figured was an acceptable amount of surprise. "You read them."

"Cover to cover. It took three days and a good part of three nights. It was the most time I've spent with my father since I was a kid."

The sound of elderly laughter carried from the front of the store. Henry must have been telling one of the many jokes he shared with his customers throughout the day.

Claire moved a bit closer to Fletcher, still without touching him. She wished suddenly that she'd grown up here, with a father like Henry and a mother the way she imagined Henry's wife, helping out in the bakery, surrounded by comforting food and comforting laughter, listening to sweet silly jokes and feeling safe. Feeling secure in her own world might have emboldened her now.

She reached out as far as she dared. "How was it, the time with your father?"

Fletcher pushed a hand through his hair. "Different. I discovered some things. He loved my mother."

The revelation emerged on a tide of pain, but it was a different pain than she'd seen in him before.

"He wrote a lot about the way Jule was when they first met. Vivacious and outgoing. He said she was the most beautiful woman he'd ever seen." Fletcher hesitated, but only a moment. "The year I turned three, he wrote that her mental illness came between them. That it was breaking him."

Ice-cold shock pulled Claire's muscles like a drawstring. "Your mother had a mental illness?"

Fletcher nodded, so slightly she almost missed it. "I remember the fun. The crazy, all-night adventures. The big emotions. Anything negative I attributed to her unhappy marriage, but he described it…from another perspective."

Planting the heel of his hand on the work counter, as if for support, Fletcher said, "My father was a doctor who was American Medical Association all the way. He took my mother to a shrink who diagnosed her as manic-depressive.

Today it's called bipolar. Victor writes about wanting Jule to take medication, and how she hated the side effects. It sounds like she took it when he was there to supervise, but skipped every chance she got. According to him, it became the main topic of their fights."

Questions began to chase each other through Claire's head. She caught one and voiced it. "He never talked to you about your mother's illness?"

"Apparently, Jule didn't want him to. He says she begged him to keep it secret. My grandfather complied with her and put pressure on Victor to do the same." Fletcher pressed his fingers against his eyelids. "No matter how angry I was or how badly I acted out, he never breathed a word. I don't think he intended for me to see the diaries, ever. He started several entries saying that writing had become his only escape."

"But he gave them to Gwen for you to read after his death."

Fletcher shook his head. "She found them when she went through his things." The blue-gray eyes that could turn so cold now overflowed with regret. "Gwen and Victor turned to each other for help when my mom was out of control. When their relationship became something else, they let guilt stop them for a while, but…" He rubbed the back of his neck. "I've judged them for so long, it's become a habit."

"A habit you want to break?"

"She loved him. She left because she didn't want to break up a family, and he let her go because of the guilt. And because his younger son was a pain in the ass who consumed all his time. Jule had begged him not to divorce her. He agreed because he was afraid of what would happen to me. Gwen was younger than Victor. She married someone else, had a child of her own, but Victor loved her the rest of his life."

Spontaneously, Claire touched Fletcher's hand, a silent

entreaty not to spend any more time than he had to stumbling down a road filled with regrets.

He turned his hand palm up, squeezing her fingers. "They spent his last two years as best friends, and maybe something more. I don't know. He doesn't say, and I'm not going to ask her. The diary entries were sporadic over the past several years, but the final entry puts his will into perspective. It was written a year before he died. He wrote that if he had his life to live over, and if there were only one thing he could do differently, he'd have hung on to Gwen *'with both my hands and all my heart. Because that one thing might have changed everything.'*"

He entwined his fingers with Claire's. "I'm a selfish S.O.B., Claire. If you're smart, you'll call Mr. Berns to come in with his rolling pin." He reached for her other hand, too, and held tightly while he spoke without a filter to censor his feelings. "I don't want to spend the rest of my life missing you."

Heart beating too fast and too hard, Claire tried to pull her hand away. "Our ten minutes are up," she told him, not ungently. "I'm glad Gwen reached out to you. Glad you read the diaries. But…"

She tried again to remove her hands from his, but he wasn't ready to let go.

"Hear me out." Tension roughened Fletcher's request. He exhaled on a hard sigh. "For the first time, I understand my father. He wanted to be a better man than he was. A better husband, a better father. But he got lost between the wanting and the doing."

Raising their clasped hands, he pressed his lips to her knuckles. "I can't be the man I want to be unless you're with me—in my mind, in my bed, in my life. No man can be his best when the biggest part, the strongest part of his heart is gone. Claire I—"

"Stop!"

Emotion pulsed through Claire like a wild river, deep and uncontrolled. Nothing was simple with Fletcher. Nothing ever would be. Suddenly, though, everything seemed clear.

Over the past year, she had learned to stand on her own. With no adult family to cushion the sometimes-terrifying aloneness, she had been forced to dig deep for courage.

Knowing exactly what she had to say, she extricated herself from Fletcher's grasp and reached now into her well of resolve. "You've been a friend to me this fall. A very good, unexpected friend. And you've been a wonderful lover. For a while you chased my nighttime fears away. But it's winter now, and I won't lie to myself. Warm arms and friendship aren't enough. Even love isn't enough."

Fletcher's brows swooped together. She felt his anxiety and his desire to speak again, but overrode it. "I'm not the woman you're talking about. I'm not like Gwen. She sacrificed herself in the end. She gave your father up when it was the right thing to do."

Holding Fletcher's gaze, she shook her head slowly and with finality. Her legs felt weak and wobbly. She could make this point only once.

"I've sacrificed myself one way or another all my life. First by pretending I didn't mind acting like a mother when really all I wanted was to be somebody's daughter. And then—"

She stopped and took a breath. This next part was the hardest to say. She wanted it to come out right.

"With Arlo, I thought all my dreams were coming true. And they did, for that time. But I was dreaming of security then, of feeling like I truly belonged somewhere, with someone. I didn't even think to dream about a love that could turn me upside down or make me feel like I belonged not only to the man, but...to the earth and the sky and to everybody I see. I guess that's what true love does. It wakes you up and connects you to everything. Maybe that would have scared me too much back then."

This time it was she who reached for his hands. She who raised them to her lips.

"It doesn't scare me anymore, Fletcher. It's what I want. I can't be strong and self-sacrificing, because I know what having soul mate feels like now, and I won't take anything else. So if you're going to say, *I love you, Claire,* then you need to add *And I intend this to be forever, for the rest of our lives, no matter what happens,* because, Fletcher Kingsley, if you say I love you, then I'm never going to let you go."

The gray-blue winter in Fletcher's eyes filled with rain clouds one last time. A few tears fell and then summer came, a sky-blue summer that told Claire what she needed to know even before he crushed her to him.

"I love you, Claire." He rasped the vow against her mouth just before he began to kiss her. "I do love you, and I love those magnificent kids of yours. I will for the rest of our lives. Forever. No matter what."

They let go of their own hearts then and held each other's. Fletcher kissed Claire with the exquisite passion of someone who had lived his life for the sole purpose of arriving at this moment. She returned the feeling, wrapping him in her arms, making a permanent place for him.

And as they stood together, past the end of Claire's coffee break, whispering promises of always, the kitchen of the old bakery filled with a love that was sweeter than honey.

## *Epilogue*

The first bars of Faith Hill's "This Kiss" filled the lavishly decorated Honeyford Community Center. Enthusiastically interpreted by Crystallized Honey, a five-piece band that, until tonight, hadn't played at a wedding since 1992, the song brought the crowd to their feet in the old public hall.

Fletcher gazed into a pair of liquid hazel eyes and requested, "What do you say, gorgeous? May I have this dance?"

"Mmmmm-AAH!" Rosalind responded, pinching her brand new stepfather's nose, then turning to wave her chubby fists at the dancers.

Fletcher laughed, grabbing one of Rozzy's hands and bouncing to the music. He slowed to a gentle sway when the baby twisted in his arms, trying to locate her mother.

"She's right over there—" he directed Rosalind's attention to the woman in the middle of the pack of dancers "—with your brothers and Zayde Henry. See her?"

In a floor-length pine-green gown that coordinated with the Christmas theme of their wedding, Claire looked stunning—glowing with confidence and joy—as she danced in a circle with three of the men in her life. Gabriella, from the Honey Comb Barbershop, had tucked tiny pearl-like beads into Claire's hair, but Fletcher knew his wife's beauty was an inside job.

Not forty-five minutes before, Zayde Henry had walked her down the aisle of the Little Chapel, where Fletcher had waited with Dean, Will and Orlando, all in matching suits, by his side. Never had he meant any words more than the vow he had taken tonight to love, honor and cherish this family of his, every moment for the rest of his life.

As he and Rosalind watched, Orlando began to run in place, his knees pumping like pistons, and Claire tossed her head back to laugh. Then she raised the hem of her gown and tried the same crazy step.

"Mmm-ma-ma!" Rosalind squealed, clapping her hands.

Fletcher kissed his stepdaughter's cheek. "I'm with you, kiddo. I can't take my eyes off her, either." He whispered into her tiny ear. "There's nobody like your mama."

No one else who could make him so sure that he was finally right where he was supposed to be.

"There's my dolly!" Irene Gould approached with her arms outstretched. Rosalind immediately leaned toward the woman she knew as "Bubbe," and Fletcher settled his daughter in the older woman's arms. The crowd on the dance floor sent up a sudden cheer, and they turned to see Zayde Henry doing the Charleston, his wiry arms and legs giving Orlando's and Will's a run for the money.

"That *meshugenah* showoff is going to break a hip,"

Irene predicted. "He just told Lucy Simms that he can still do handstands." She shook her head. Pursing her lips at the baby, she cooed, "Never mind him, you angel. Come. Bubbe wants to show you off to her friends." Blowing a coral-lipped kiss to Fletcher, she set off with the baby on a tour of the room.

Fletcher decided to claim his bride for a slow dance, no matter what the next song was, but he'd only taken a couple of steps when he heard a calm, cordial voice. "It was a beautiful ceremony. Thank you for inviting me."

Looking down, he saw Gwen Gibson standing next to him, a glass of garishly bright punch in her hands. He smiled. Easily. "Thanks for coming."

He could tell Gwen had something on her mind and reluctantly settled for watching his wife from the sidelines a bit longer. Turning toward the woman he had accepted as his ally rather than his enemy in past few weeks, he said, "Claire's been telling everyone who'll listen that this is a marriage of convenience. She thinks it's romantic." He allowed his expression to tell her how he felt about that.

Gwen's attractive face grew troubled. "But you signed away all your rights to the ranch. You can't inherit it now."

"She's not telling people that I had to marry her. She's saying she had to marry me so Henry will make her a partner in the bakery. She claims he wants it to be run by a married couple."

"Is that true?"

"I don't think so. But she's enjoying herself so much, I hate to out her."

Gwen smiled. She looked particularly attractive this evening in a crimson velvet blazer and long black skirt, and Fletcher told her so.

Her cheeks turned red, and she took a sip of her punch before thanking him. "I don't see you baking cookies for a living," she ventured.

Fletcher laughed. "No."

"Any plans?"

He nodded. "We're staying here, I know that. Now that I've had time to think about what I *really* want, I'm going forward with the plans for a horse ranch. I appreciate the city allowing me to keep my stock at Pine Road until I find another spread."

Intent on marrying Claire well within the time prescription of his father's will, Fletcher had told his lawyers to draw up papers relinquishing his claim to the ranch. No way would he have anyone questioning his desire to be her husband, or the father to her children. *Their* children. His wife had protested vociferously, and although he knew he was going to spend the better part of his life saying yes to any request she made, on this he had refused. She'd told him he was being ridiculous. And then she'd begun to spread the word that she was marrying him to get the bakery.

Grinning, Fletcher checked his watch. How much more socializing before they could start the honeymoon?

Beside him, Gwen cleared her throat uncomfortably. "Um, I have a small confession." Fletcher raised a brow, and she offered a weak smile. "When I heard you were back in town and that you'd moved into the ranch house, I got this idea." She winced. "It was an absurd idea, it didn't even make any sense, really, but I knew you'd be furious about the marriage mandate in Victor's will and would try to find a way out of it, and I also knew how much it meant to your father that you find a good woman, and so…" She raised the punch to her lips then made a face as if it were sour rather than sweet.

"Sorry, Gwen, I'm not following you." Crystallized Honey had begun a slow number, and he wanted to claim his wife.

"I put that insane ad in the paper, and I knew the moment I did it that it was absurd. Anyone could have answered that ad. A seventy-year-old could have. But…I think things turned out well, and I hope you'll forgive me for meddling?"

Gwen looked at Fletcher with pleading, apologetic eyes. He felt as if he'd taken a hoof to the head.

"*You* put the ad—the one Claire answered—in *The Buzz*?"

She nodded. "It wasn't very mayorly. It wasn't even very sane. I'm not sure what came over me, and if you tell Claire, I hope you'll both—"

She stopped talking as Fletcher's laughter drowned out her words, and his arms came around her. Punch sloshed out of her cup.

When he was done hugging, Fletcher kissed her on the cheek. "Are you going to put an ad in the paper for Dean, too?"

Clearly confused but relieved by Fletcher's reaction, she nonetheless blanched at his suggestion. "No, of course not!"

"I'm surrounded by reckless women."

They stood awhile, smiling at each other, and then Gwen said, "Do you have a dollar?"

The request seemed to come out of nowhere, but Fletcher told himself to surrender to the unexpected. Reaching for his billfold, he handed Gwen her dollar. "Do you need more?"

"No, this will do." She tucked the bill into the pocket of her blazer. "We'll send everything to the title company Monday morning."

"What?"

"The city council decided unanimously to sell Pine Road Ranch for 'the best offer' before seven p.m. tonight, and you just made it." She patted her pocket. "Thank you very much. Oh, look! Henry Berns is trying to do the worm." Before Fletcher could say a word, Gwen blended into the crowd of dancers.

*I'll be damned.*

Maybe someday he would learn how to balance now that the earth, as he'd known it, had tipped on its axis, but tonight he felt decidedly off-kilter.

Claire approached, flushed and grinning and glorious, and Fletcher shook his head. The hell with balance; it was highly overrated.

"It's almost time to cut the cake." She planted a full, but much-too-quick kiss on his eager lips. "Now remember, you promised not to smash it all over me. The bakery has never done wedding cakes before, and this is our advertising." She smoothed his tie then placed her soft palm against his cheek. "Telling people I had to marry you to become a partner has turned out to be great publicity. Can you imagine?" She grinned, full of spice. "People think it's romantic."

"With you, I can imagine anything." He gathered her to him, his hands wandering too close to her bottom in a public setting, but whatever. He bent closer and closer to kiss her exactly the way he wanted to, and she stretched up just as eagerly, but before their lips made contact, he said, "Unfortunately for the bakery, I just took back the ranch, and even though I paid good money for it, some folks are bound to say *I* married *you* out of convenience."

Her eyes went wide and delighted. "Fletcher! You got your ranch? That's—mmm…"

They melted into a kiss, melted into each other's bodies, melted into each other's hearts. He pulled back. "*Our* ranch," he murmured then kissed her some more.

As one by one the good folks of Honeyford turned to watch and smile, they all suspected the truth, anyway: that tonight they had witnessed not a marriage of convenience, but the joining of souls. And that what love had started, nothing in this world could ever end.

\* \* \* \* \*

*Don't miss Dean Kingsley's story,*
*coming soon, wherever Silhouette Books are sold.*

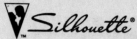

# COMING NEXT MONTH

## Available September 28, 2010

SPECIAL EDITION

# REQUEST YOUR FREE BOOKS!
## 2 FREE NOVELS PLUS 2 FREE GIFTS!

# SPECIAL EDITION
### Life, Love and Family!

**YES!** Please send me 2 FREE Silhouette® Special Edition® novels and my 2 FREE gifts (gifts are worth about $10). After receiving them, if I don't wish to receive any more books, I can return the shipping statement marked "cancel." If I don't cancel, I will receive 6 brand-new novels every month and be billed just $4.24 per book in the U.S. or $4.99 per book in Canada. That's a saving of 15% off the cover price! It's quite a bargain! Shipping and handling is just 50¢ per book.* I understand that accepting the 2 free books and gifts places me under no obligation to buy anything. I can always return a shipment and cancel at any time. Even if I never buy another book from Silhouette, the two free books and gifts are mine to keep forever.

235/335 SDN E5RG

| | | |
|---|---|---|
| Name | (PLEASE PRINT) | |
| Address | | Apt. # |
| City | State/Prov. | Zip/Postal Code |

Signature (if under 18, a parent or guardian must sign)

### Mail to the **Silhouette Reader Service:**
**IN U.S.A.:** P.O. Box 1867, Buffalo, NY 14240-1867
**IN CANADA:** P.O. Box 609, Fort Erie, Ontario L2A 5X3

Not valid for current subscribers to Silhouette Special Edition books.

**Want to try two free books from another line?**
**Call 1-800-873-8635 or visit www.morefreebooks.com.**

* Terms and prices subject to change without notice. Prices do not include applicable taxes. N.Y. residents add applicable sales tax. Canadian residents will be charged applicable provincial taxes and GST. Offer not valid in Quebec. This offer is limited to one order per household. All orders subject to approval. Credit or debit balances in a customer's account(s) may be offset by any other outstanding balance owed by or to the customer. Please allow 4 to 6 weeks for delivery. Offer available while quantities last.

**Your Privacy:** Silhouette is committed to protecting your privacy. Our Privacy Policy is available online at www.eHarlequin.com or upon request from the Reader Service. From time to time we make our lists of customers available to reputable third parties who may have a product or service of interest to you. If you would prefer we not share your name and address, please check here. ☐

**Help us get it right**—We strive for accurate, respectful and relevant communications. To clarify or modify your communication preferences, visit us at www.ReaderService.com/consumerschoice.

SSE10R

# HARLEQUIN®

## A Romance

## FOR EVERY MOOD™

Spotlight on

## Inspirational

Wholesome romances
that touch the heart and soul.

See the next page
to enjoy a sneak peek from
the Love Inspired® inspirational series.

*See below for a sneak peek at*
*our inspirational line, Love Inspired®.*
*Introducing HIS HOLIDAY BRIDE*
*by bestselling author Jillian Hart*

Autumn Granger gave her horse rein to slide toward the town's new sheriff.

"Hey, there." The man in a brand-new Stetson, black T-shirt, jeans and riding boots held up a hand in greeting. He stepped away from his four-wheel drive with "Sheriff" in black on the doors and waded through the grasses. "I'm new around here."

"I'm Autumn Granger."

"Nice to meet you, Miss Granger. I'm Ford Sherman, from Chicago." He knuckled back his hat, revealing the most handsome face she'd ever seen. Big blue eyes contrasted with his sun-tanned complexion.

"I'm guessing you haven't seen much open land. Out here, you've got to keep an eye on cows or they're going to tear your vehicle apart."

"What?" He whipped around. Sure enough, mammoth black-and-white creatures had started to gnaw on his four-wheel drive. They clustered like a mob, mouths and tongues and teeth bent on destruction. One cow tried to pry the wiper off the windshield, another chewed on the side mirror. Several leaned through the open window, licking the seats.

"Move along, little dogie." He didn't know the first thing about cattle.

The entire herd swiveled their heads to study him curiously. Not a single hoof shifted. The animals soon returned to chewing, licking, digging through his possessions.

Autumn laughed, a warm and wonderful sound. "Thanks,

I needed that." She then pulled a bag from behind her saddle and waved it at the cows. "Look what I have, guys. Cookies."

Cows swung in her direction, and dozens of liquid brown eyes brightened with cookie hopes. As she circled the car, the cattle bounded after her. The earth shook with the force of their powerful hooves.

"Next time, you're on your own, city boy." She tipped her hat. The cowgirl stayed on his mind, the sweetest thing he had ever seen.

*Will Ford be able to stick it out in the country
to find out more about Autumn?
Find out in HIS HOLIDAY BRIDE
by bestselling author Jillian Hart,
available in October 2010
only from Love Inspired®.*

# BARBARA HANNAY

*A Miracle for His Secret Son*

Freya and Gus shared a perfect summer, until Gus left town for a future that couldn't include Freya.... Now eleven years on, Freya has a life-changing revelation for Gus: they have a son, Nick, who needs a new kidney—a gift only his father can provide. Gus is stunned by the news, but vows to help Nick. And despite everything, Gus realizes that he still loves Freya.

**Can they forge a future together and give Nick another miracle...a family?**

*Available October 2010*